P9-CCO-472

Other Clarion Books by
MARION DANE BAUER

Rain of Fire
Tangled Butterfly
Foster Child
Shelter From the Wind

Like Mother,
Like Daughter

Like Mother, Like Daughter

Marion Dane Bauer

CLARION BOOKS

TICKNOR & FIELDS: A HOUGHTON MIFFLIN COMPANY

NEW YORK

Clarion Books
Ticknor & Fields, a Houghton Mifflin Company

Library of Congress Cataloging in Publication Data
Bauer, Marion Dane.
    Like mother, like daughter.
    Summary: Leslie has trouble relating to her mother and turns instead to
her new journalism advisor at school, until a moment of crisis puts a different
perspective on things.
    [1. Mothers and daughters—Fiction. 2. Teacher-student relationships—
Fiction. 3. Schools—Fiction]
I. Title.
PZ7.B3262Li 1985   [Fic]   85–479
ISBN 0–89919–356–0

s 10 9 8 7 6 5 4 3 2

For my mother and my daughter,
of course,
but also, and especially,
for Emily Crofford,
who is neither
and both.

Like Mother,
Like Daughter

One

The day I stood in the middle of a public park and watched my mother giving artificial respiration to a cat was the day I made the most important decision of my life.

I decided that I was going to grow up to be as different from my mother as it is possible to be.

I may look like her—mouse-brown hair and no-particular-color eyes that she calls hazel and the kind of tall, skinny body designed to disappear behind telephone poles—but looks I can't do much about. The part I *can* control is how I act. There are a lot of things I still don't know about how I want to be, but I can tell you one thing for sure. The drowning cats of this world might as well take notice. They aren't going to get any help from me.

It was a mid-October day when it happened. My mother and my best friend, Kate Connolly, and I were out for our annual autumn-leaves camp-out. We live in a suburb of Minneapolis, and though there are plenty of leaves at home to see—and plenty to rake, too—the three of us go out every year for one last time when the fall color is at its peak. (My dad and my kid brother, Brian, stay home. This is always strictly a female outing.)

We were camping on the St. Croix River. Most people come to Minnesota to vacation on the lakes, but my mother prefers rivers. She says they have more character. Anyway, we were sitting around a late-afternoon campfire roasting marshmallows, competing to see who could toast theirs to perfection. Your marshmallow was eliminated if it caught fire or turned black or went limp and slid off the stick. A perfect marshmallow, in case you don't know, is crisp and light brown on the outside and entirely liquid goo in the middle.

Suddenly my mother leaped up. "Leslie, did you see that?" she cried.

"See what?" Kate and I asked, jumping up too.

"That man! Upstream there. He threw a gunny-sack into the river, and I'm certain it had something live in it."

Kate and I stared in the direction my mother was pointing, but all I could see was the tip of something brown bobbling along in the river. Whatever it was didn't appear worth getting excited about.

My mother, however, had already dropped her marshmallow stick and kicked off her shoes. Before I could say a word to stop her, she had also stepped out of her jeans and headed for the river.

I didn't want to look. Just imagine it. There was my mother in drooping pink panties and an old shirt of my dad's, wading into the St. Croix River after a ... who knew what it was? Maybe the guy was drowning a skunk ... or a rat ... or his garbage. My mother never sees possibilities like that, though. Sometimes, when she goes into action, I don't think she even sees.

By the time she emerged from the river, dripping and carrying the sack, some people who were fishing nearby had begun to gather around. And there was my mother, half-naked, tearing at the knot in the top of the gunnysack.

"I need a knife," she ordered, and someone supplied a knife. She took to sawing, and pretty soon she pulled out the wettest, scraggliest, skinniest-looking black cat I've ever seen. It hung in her arms like a wet rag, apparently dead.

Everybody started saying "Isn't it too bad?" and drifting away the way people do. Only they didn't know my mother. She doesn't quit so easily. She knelt down, right there on the edge of the river, and pressed on the cat's chest until some water spewed out of his mouth, and then—like I've already said— she bent over and started to give that mangy beast mouth to mouth.

"Gross!" some little kids yelled. "Yuck!" Even Kate paled and turned around very quickly and walked back to the fire.

I just stood there, unable to move.

"Mother," I said, "what if he's sick or something? What if he has rabies?" I could imagine the cat, and then my mother, foaming at the mouth. But she didn't stop. I guess I knew she wouldn't. After a while I walked back up to the campfire too, and stood pretending to warm myself, though my face was burning.

"I'm sorry," I said to Kate. "But you know my mother."

"You don't need to be sorry," Kate said.

We waited there by the fire for what seemed like forever before my mother joined us, the limp cat pressed against her chest. "He's breathing," she whispered, as if she were afraid she might startle the creature with the news. "He's going to live!"

"That's wonderful, Mrs. Johnson," Kate said, and she touched the triangular black head with a tentative finger.

"Just what we need at our house," I added, "another cat." After all, we only had three already, not to mention three dogs, all of them rescued from the pound or from some equally awful fate.

Mom was busy wrapping the ugly, skinny thing in towels—Kate's and my towels as well as her own. "It's too bad," she was saying, "but we'll have to go home. He'll need to be kept warm . . . and to be fed, with an eyedropper, probably. And I'd better talk to the vet to see what I should do if he develops pneumonia."

"What will we do if you develop pneumonia?" I

asked, holding up her jeans, and she gave me a crooked smile. I think it was the first moment she realized she wasn't exactly fully dressed.

"Thanks, Leslie," she said, and she held the bundle out for me to take.

"Mom!" I said, exasperated, but she continued to stand there, her expression pleasant and reasonable, somehow, as though it were the most ordinary part of any day to ask somebody to hold a half-dead cat. I held out my arms woodenly, and she laid the cat across them.

Even through the layers of towel, I could feel his wavering breaths. I studied his face. It was narrow, almost pointed in the manner of a highly bred Siamese, though his black fur was pure alley cat. He glared at me through slitted blue eyes. "The feeling is mutual, cat," I said under my breath.

When my mother had pulled on her jeans and poked her muddy feet into her sneakers, I handed the bundle back without comment.

"I'm afraid this spoils the weekend, but I don't know what else I can do under the circumstances," she said.

"I know you don't." I tried to sound sympathetic.

It didn't matter about having to go home early. When you're nearly fifteen (I'll be fifteen next spring, anyway) you're almost too old for camping with your mother anyway.

Kate and I took down the tent and packed the gear while Mother crooned to the swaddled cat in her arms, and when we were ready to go, he got the place of honor on the front seat.

"I think I'll name him Aslan," Mom said as Kate and I climbed into the back.

"Aslan!" I repeated. "Isn't he the lion from the Narnia stories, the one who represents Jesus?"

"Sure." Mom smiled at me in the rearview mirror. "After all, this cat rose from the dead, didn't he?"

I could still hear Aslan's breathing, thin and rasping, and smell the chicken-feather stench of wet fur. "I guess he didn't have much choice," I said.

. . .

"How's Aslan?" Kate asked me when I flopped into the chair next to her in the school library on Monday.

I groaned. "Don't ask."

"Why not?"

"Unfortunately, it looks like he's going to survive."

"Oh, come on, Leslie," she said. "You know you're going to love that cat as much as you love the rest of your family zoo."

"No, I'm not. He's the most obnoxious animal I've ever seen. He goes around hissing at everything that gets into his way, table legs, walls, you name it."

"He's probably just scared." Kate's voice was meant to be soothing, but I was feeling annoyed.

"He has good reason to be scared. Every time I look at him do you know what I think of? My mother kneeling on that riverbank in her underpants. It makes me want to finish the job that guy started."

Kate gave me her patient look, the look she saves for times when she thinks I'm being unreasonable. Sometimes I don't know why we're such good friends. Kate is quiet and sensible, and I'm forever flying off loudly in one direction or the other. "Try to think before you erupt," my father says sometimes, but I never do.

"It wasn't so bad," Kate said. "Really!"

I slammed a book onto the table so hard that Mrs. Seneca, the librarian, looked our way and scowled. "I noticed *you* didn't stand around very long to watch," I said.

Kate ducked her head and said nothing more. Around us there was the undercurrent of buzz and clamor that you always get in a place where junior high kids are supposed to be quiet.

"I'm serious, Kate. I really am! I've had enough of living with the local bleeding heart. If it's not animals, it's foster kids or exchange students—Did you know that one time my mother met a bag lady on the bus and brought her home?

"A real bag lady?" Even Kate looked surprised.

"A real bag lady. Her name was Hannah or Hilda or something like that. She stayed for three nights, ate our food, complained about Brian's and my table manners, and then went back to living on the street."

"Only your mother," Kate said, but she was smiling the way people do when my mother is the topic of conversation. "A saint," some of the people at church call her, but they always say it in a way that makes it clear they're glad *she's* the saint and not them.

Mrs. Seneca was now giving us meaningful looks, so I leaned closer to Kate and whispered, "Do you know what scares me? I mean really scares me?"

She turned her palms up to show that she didn't know.

"I'm afraid I might grow up to be *like* her!"

Kate leaned close to me to answer. "That wouldn't be so bad, Leslie. Really!"

"Not so bad!" I exploded with such force that Mrs. Seneca was instantly at our table, her pencil tapping.

"Now, what's this, girls? Don't you have some work to do?" she asked, all proper and snooty.

"We *have* to talk," I said, trying to sound businesslike, "because we have to work together. Our column for *The Roving Reporter* is due today."

Kate nodded her agreement, and the fact was that we did write the gossip column for *The Roving Reporter*, our school newspaper. You know the kind of stuff. "Is there anybody who *hasn't* seen DY and TM skulking around the parking lot during lunch? How long do you suppose it will be before SB catches on?"

"Well, then you'd better get to work, hadn't you?" Mrs. Seneca said, her voice that kind of artificial sweet meant not to hide a threat.

"Yes, ma'am," Kate said, and Mrs. Seneca moved on to the next table, her pencil still going.

Kate rolled her eyes, pushed a strand of long, dark hair away from her face, and we both waited in silence until Mrs. Seneca had tapped her way to the other side of the library.

I glared at Kate then and hissed, "You can't be serious. If I thought I was going to grow up to be like my mother, I think I'd shoot myself."

Kate studied my face. "Do you mean it, Leslie?"

"I've never meant anything more."

"It's funny." She was shaking her head. "When I was a little kid, I used to wish that my mother was like yours. In fact, I used to pretend that I was adopted, that your mother was the one who'd really had me."

My mouth fell open. Kate's mother is a high-powered attorney and president of the Board of Education, her father an executive of some kind. Kate's an only child, and she and her parents go skiing at Vail every Christmas and have been to Europe twice. Talk about trading a silk purse for a sow's ear! All I could think to say, though, was "Can you imagine my mother having a baby and giving it away? She can't even get rid of a scraggly cat."

Kate shrugged.

"You should have known better, anyway," I added. "Our birthdays are only two months apart."

Kate looked at me and smiled. "So . . . I was a dumb little kid."

Mrs. Seneca was moving back up toward the front of the library. We fell silent again, and I riffled through my French book, trying to look busy. I couldn't comprehend Kate's envying me *my* mother, though. I mean her mother is one of those people who does everything perfectly. She comes home from work and changes into designer jeans to fix creamed chicken in puffed pastry shells. One of my mother's better clothing combinations is a red sweat shirt with purple pants, and she's the kind of cook who puts garbanzo beans in everything from salad to apple pie. She also forgets, every time she picks up the Tabasco sauce, that nobody in our family likes things hot—not even her.

And you should see Kate's house! Not even a full-time housekeeper could make ours look like that. When I was a little kid, I used to think it was convenient to find Oreos beneath the couch cushions and to feed the cats on the kitchen counter to keep their food away from the dogs. Now I just think it's gross.

"Do you remember the party your mom put on for your tenth birthday, Leslie?"

"Yeah . . . sure," I answered. For my tenth birthday my mother had started my party in the observatory at the top of the IDS building in downtown Minneapolis and ended it in St. Paul. We'd all climbed out onto the roof of the state capitol where the gold horses are and eaten hot dogs and Twinkies that we had bought from a vendor. The guard came and chased us down, saying we weren't supposed to bring food up there.

I remembered other things, too . . . like the time

my mother came and took me out of school for no reason except that we'd just had our first deep snow of the winter, and she'd found a cross-country ski trail where no one had yet laid a ski. Or the way she used to act out all the characters and voices when she read to Brian and me, or her letting me bake my mud pies in her oven.

I sighed. "I'm not saying my mother's a bad person or anything like that. I just don't want to *be* her. Can you understand that?"

Kate nodded, but I still wasn't convinced that she understood.

"People are always telling us how much we look alike," I said, "and then they turn around and tell me how wonderful she is. Sometimes I get . . . well, scared. I can't do the things she does, Kate. I mean, I don't even want to. But sometimes I think maybe there's no other way for me to be."

Kate looked sympathetic then. "What you need," she said in an authoritative voice she doesn't often use, "is a female role model. Remember how Miss Nelson used to talk about role models all the time."

"Miss Nelson!" I giggled. She had been the adviser for our school paper, and she had said a lot of things, most of it nonsense. At the end of her first month of teaching she had decided she was in the wrong career—which is something we could have told her the first day—and resigned.

"Girls!" Mrs. Seneca interrupted, her pencil drumming the table again. "You're still chattering!"

"No, ma'am," I answered. "We're not. We're discussing."

Mrs. Seneca's pencil skipped a beat. For a moment she held her ground, trying to stare me down, but when I returned her look in kind, she moved away without saying more, her back end tight and prissy.

"Still," I said to Kate, "I don't suppose even Miss Nelson was wrong about everything. A role model might help. I wonder, though, where a person finds such a thing in a joint like this?"

Kate looked around and shook her head. "You might consider asking your mother to bring home another bag lady," she said.

Two

eciding you're going to find a role model and finding one are two different things. I looked in every corner of my life for the next week— fortunately there weren't any bag ladies to check out—but I couldn't find anyone I wanted to be even a little bit like. A couple of my teachers were okay, but I knew by the time I was ten that I didn't want to be a teacher. (My father teaches the fifth grade, so I know how hard they have to work and how little they earn.)

Then came the day that Kate and I walked into *The Roving Reporter* staff room seventh hour and met our new adviser. We came sauntering in not expecting anything different, not expecting anything at all, really. We'd had a substitute for about a month, a funny old lady who never did anything but sit behind her desk and read romance novels (which she tried to hide behind a *Webster's Dictionary*) while we put out the newspaper. She never tried to teach us a thing. She didn't even check the copy before it went to the printer. Not that Miss Nelson had taught us much or checked the copy too carefully either, for all of her talk about role models.

That's why, I guess, that Dr. Schultz, our principal, had been looking for someone with "actual newspaper experience" to fill Miss Nelson's place. It's what he'd told us, anyway, and we all figured it would take him a while to locate a teacher with qualifications like that. The minute we walked through the door, though, I knew it had been worth the wait.

Our new adviser stood there, a giant of a woman, taller than me, taller, even, than my mother. She had cinnamon-colored hair that she'd pulled back into a French twist, very businesslike, and she was wearing frameless, sort of octagonal glasses and a softly tailored suit. But the glasses couldn't hide her eyes—they were pale blue, the palest eyes I've ever seen—and the suit couldn't hide her figure. It was . . . well, it was exactly what you would want a figure to be. One of the boys coming in behind me whistled through his teeth when he hit the door.

We all stopped in a clump, just inside the room, feeling like intruders and waiting for her to notice that we were there. There were nine of us on the staff, so it would have been a little hard for her not to notice. She, however, was reading the latest issue of *The Roving Reporter*, and she went on reading just as though she were alone in the room.

When she had read every last word, even the ads on the back page, she dropped the paper on the desk in front of her, looked from one to the other of us with eyes so sharp they could pin a mosquito to the wall, and asked, in a resonating voice, "Who's been editing this crap?"

Nobody breathed. Nobody answered, either.

"Come on, now," she demanded. "I'm sure it's not a revelation from God which appears mysteriously on paper twice a month." She picked the offending pages up and slapped them against the desk several times. I could feel myself wincing with every sharp crack our little paper made against the metal desk.

"I guess we've never actually had an editor," one boy volunteered at last when her look skewered him again. I didn't know him very well except that his name was Dave. He was pretty much a loner. He was also about four inches shorter than me, and he dressed punk, as out of date as punk was: feathered earrings, Easter-egg-colored hair, the works. He looked like a bantam cock standing there.

The woman looked Dave up and down with considerable thoroughness—apparently she hadn't noticed him before he spoke, and then she put her head back and laughed. She had the longest, whitest throat I have ever seen away from a movie screen.

"You guess you've never had an editor?" she

repeated, the laugh fading quickly and an incredulous look taking its place. And then she added, "You seem to be the only person with the courage to speak up. What's your name?"

"Dave," he responded. "Dave Wiley."

She nodded abruptly and turned back to the rest of us. Kate had been easing behind me the whole time, trying to disappear, I could tell.

The adviser fixed her gaze on me. "What's your name, and what do you do?" she demanded.

"My name's Leslie Johnson," I answered, my voice shaking embarrassingly. I don't know what I thought this Amazon was going to do, pound bamboo stakes beneath my thumbnails? "And I write the gossip column."

"Gossip column!" she repeated. "This entire paper is little more than a gossip column."

She stood glaring at all of us for a moment, and then she began to pace, back and forth, like a tigress in a cage. Every time she got back behind her desk, she slapped the paper against the metal surface again. "Do you people realize," she asked, "that there isn't a single word . . . not a syllable of true journalism in this entire ridiculous effort? There's not a thought, not a plan, not even a passing intention. There isn't one scrap of integrity. In fact, there is nothing here but fatuous filth and"—she stared in my direction—"gossip. I'm surprised the administration has tolerated such a shoddy performance."

I could feel Kate edging toward the door. I had

talked her into signing up for the newspaper staff in the first place so we'd be sure to have one class together, but I knew this was more than she had bargained for.

"Is this what you write?" the adviser asked, suddenly squaring off against me again and stabbing the paper with a long, brilliantly polished fingernail.

"Uh, I guess so," I said.

"You guess so?" she repeated. "You mean you don't know?"

"I can't exactly see what you're pointing to," I replied, my voice faint.

The woman picked the paper up and read with exaggerated emphasis, "A little bird told us that BD and ML have been seen 'studying' together in the library. If that's studying, then grades are chocolate kisses!"

It was definitely Kate's and my gossip column she was talking about—what I had considered one of my more brilliant inventions the week before, and I swallowed with some difficulty. "Yes, ma'am. I did," I said, figuring I'd better cover for Kate before she fainted or something worse.

Barbara Stein contributed helpfully, "Kate Connolly and Leslie write the gossip column together."

I don't know how the adviser knew who Kate was—there were half a dozen other staff kids standing around gaping—but she figured it out. Her next look sizzled across me and settled on Kate, who was almost completely behind me by this point. "You mean it took two people to write this rubbish?" she demanded.

Kate stammered, "Yes, ma'am. I mean, no, ma'am. I mean, we didn't mean to write garbage . . . or rubbish . . . or whatever you said. We just wanted . . ." Her voice faded away.

"Wanted what?" the woman demanded, returning to me.

I didn't know what we'd wanted. After all, what is there to want when you are writing a gossip column, except to please your friends and take an occasional poke at someone you don't especially like? I shrugged, remembering an old axiom of my father's, "When you have nothing to say, keep your mouth shut."

Behind me, Kate made a small noise like a canary strangling.

"They wanted," Dave squared his shoulders and stepped forward, all five feet four of him, "to write something the kids would actually read. The kids like to look for their initials in the gossip column."

For a moment everyone in the room stood frozen, like in the old game of Statues. I was sure this giant was going to step over her desk and squash Dave like an impertinent bug, but she didn't. She just looked at him, her eyes bright with some joke we hadn't been told, and then she laughed. Two loud guffaws. She reached out and took Dave's hand, just picked it up from where it hung limply at his side, and shook it vigorously.

"I like that," she said. "I really do. A little journalistic candor. How would you like to be my editor?"

Everyone in the room drew in a single breath. Dave Wiley as editor of *The Roving Reporter?* Most teachers blanched when he came into a room.

The handshake seemed to travel up Dave's arm and into his body. He jigged a couple of times on his toes, and then said, using his deepest, most authoritative voice, "Sure!"

Our new adviser smiled, dropped his hand, passed the smile around among us, and then said, "By the way, let me introduce myself. I'm Meredith Perl, *Ms.* Perl, one-time reporter for the *Chicago News*. And I'm here to teach you how to put out a real newspaper."

I don't think anybody had any idea what we were doing . . . or why, but we all cheered.

•   •   •

"Can you believe it, Kate?" I asked, as we climbed the steps to the school bus. "I've found her!"

Kate was checking her books to make sure she hadn't left anything behind. If you were Kate Connolly, the biggest disaster of the day would be forgetting some small bit of homework. I guess I haven't mentioned that Kate makes straight A's in every single course.

"Found who?" she asked, but before I could answer she added, "Didn't Mr. DeWitt give us a huge assignment in algebra?"

"That's because he forgot to give us any at all yesterday," I said. "Dim Wit's really getting senile these days. I'm going to do one day's worth, no more." I grabbed a seat and slid in toward the window. "Kate, I found my female role model . . . like we talked about."

"Oh," Kate said. "Who?"

"Ms. Perl! Who do you think?"

"Are you really only going to do part of the assignment?"

"Really. Kate . . . you're not listening to me."

Kate scowled down at her books again. The rest of the mob of kids had pushed and jostled into the aisle, and the driver snapped the door shut behind the last one. The bus lurched forward.

"I'm listening," Kate said. "Ms. Perl is going to be your female role model."

"Right."

She turned and looked at me for the first time, then asked, "Why?"

"Why?" I couldn't believe my ears. "Because she just is. She's *it*. She's the most incredible woman I've ever met. Beautiful, intelligent . . . tough. That's the way I want to be . . . really tough."

Kate shook her head, but she didn't say anything.

I was getting irritated. "What do you have against her?"

"I don't have anything against her exactly, it's just—"

"See!" I interrupted. "You don't have anything. Admit it."

Kate went back to checking out her textbooks, her face closed.

"Admit it!" I repeated, feeling as belligerent as I knew I sounded.

"Look," she said, "it's obvious you don't want to hear what I think, so why ask me?" She gazed past me out the bus window as though the gray, end-of-October day were the most fascinating thing on earth.

"Of course, I want to hear," I told her, though I knew I didn't, really. Not if she was going to say something against Ms. Perl.

Kate sighed. "It's just a feeling, Leslie. That's all."

"What kind of a feeling?" A weight was growing in the bottom of my stomach. You begin to get something sorted out and then somebody—your best friend—comes along and scrambles it for you again.

"Well, her making Dave Wiley editor for one thing . . . not even knowing him, not knowing any of us. You would have made a better editor than Dave."

For an instant that stopped me. I had never even thought of such a thing, me as editor of *The Roving Reporter*, and under Ms. Perl, no less! Before she came it wouldn't have made much difference who had the title. We had all vied to keep from being editor, in fact.

I wasn't ready to give in so easily, though. "I think it just shows that Ms. Perl can see beyond surfaces. Any other teacher would have put Dave in charge of carrying out the trash. She could see his real potential."

"Maybe," Kate conceded, "but . . ." Her voice trailed off.

"But *what*, Kate Connolly? You're driving me crazy!"

She turned to face me at last. "It seems to me she's putting on an act or something. I kept feeling like she was waiting for us to applaud."

"You're just saying that because she scares you," I said, "Now admit it. You know she does."

Kate tucked her chin inside the collar of her jacket. "I admit it. She scares me spitless. But just because I'm a coward, doesn't mean I don't know what I'm talking about. We cowards can be very perceptive, you know."

I laughed then and patted her arm. Kate was wrong. I knew she was, and I also knew she would come around eventually. That's one thing about Kate. She can always admit being wrong if she is. I rarely can. I remember when we were little how I kept insisting I *knew* there was a Santa Claus long after every one of my friends knew better, because I didn't want to admit to having been duped all those years.

"Besides," I said, "I think Dave will be a good editor."

"You know why he joined the staff, don't you? He's said it often enough."

"Yeah." I knew what Dave had said. He'd joined the staff to get out of reading *Romeo and Juliet*, which is required for ninth grade English, and I could hardly blame him for that. I wouldn't have minded getting out of it either, but my parents wouldn't let me.

It's strange. Parents and teachers tend to have fits if junior high students even date steadily, but still they make us read about these two kids—Juliet was only thirteen, did you know that?—who got married without permission from anybody. And they went through more than the ceremony, too. Of course, they died in the process. Maybe that's the point.

I turned to face Kate. "Dave's not the only kid using journalism as a substitute for ninth grade English. It's allowed, you know."

Kate couldn't dissagree with that.

"Tonight I'm going to work on the assignment Ms. Perl gave us," I said. "It'll be fun trying to figure out some issue to take on for the next paper. You want to come over and work with me?"

"If I get my algebra done," Kate said.

Algebra. Who cared about algebra? Who cared about anything old Dim Wit assigned . . . except for Kate?

The bus jerked to a stop at our corner, and we emerged into a misty rain. I tipped my face to feel the startling coolness.

"I want to come up with the best idea of anyone," I told Kate. "I'll make Ms. Perl sit up and notice me. I mean, if she's going to be my role model . . ."

Kate turned around to face me, her backpack of books held tightly against her chest. "Just be careful," she said. "Okay?"

"Careful of what?" I asked. Even I could hear the heavy sarcasm in my voice as if it were some impersonal other voice I was listening to.

Kate's sky-blue eyes never faltered from my face. "I can't tell you why, exactly, but I think Ms. Perl isn't really . . . kind."

"*Kind!*" I exploded. "What does *kind* have to do with anything? My mother is *kind.*"

"Yes," Kate said. "I know." And she turned and began the walk toward her house.

Three

"**N**ewspapers," Ms. Perl concluded, tucking her polished fingertips into the pockets of her slim skirt, "form the cornerstone of a democratic society. They provide a fourth check in the system of government checks and balances. The news media can champion the oppressed, and they can make the powerful accountable to the people. In short, good journalism, responsible journalism, daring journalism has the opportunity to change the world."

I suppose there was some response we could have made, but if there was, nobody made it. We all simply sat there, mesmerized.

Ms. Perl looked at each of us in turn. When she focused on me, it was as if she could see everything about me. What I'd eaten for breakfast, maybe, or the fact that I'd had a quarrel with Kate. It was strange, though. It was as if she saw me and knew everything about me, but she didn't make any judgment at all. It sounds dumb when I say it, but that was how it felt.

And then she capped off her whole speech, only it didn't seem like a speech, it seemed like a personal plea directed at me. "I want *The Roving Reporter* to quit playing *National Enquirer* and start being responsible to the community it's published for. I want this newspaper to make a difference. I want," she dropped her voice to a lower register so it came out with power and authority, "*you* to make a difference in this school."

Everybody nodded, even Kate. I think if Ms. Perl had been telling us to chop off our left ears we would have agreed. She was magnificent!

"Well," Dave said, standing up, looking shorter than ever beside Ms. Perl, "does anybody have an idea for our next issue?" He stood casually, one hip thrust out in a sinister way, his lip ready to curl if anyone made a stupid suggestion.

"Maybe we could run a check on what really goes into the cafeteria lunches," Jimmy Fenwick proposed.

Dave grimaced. "I'm not sure I could stomach editing the copy."

"How about an investigation of the way the cheerleaders are chosen?" Sharon Simms asked. As you might guess, Sharon tried out to be a basketball cheerleader and didn't make the squad.

Dave nodded, made a note. "You think there's something unfair about the process?"

Sharon shrugged. "I don't know. I just thought it might be worth checking."

"Okay, you can interview the judges and anyone else who has an opinion. Then let's have another article from the point of view of the cheerleaders who were chosen." He looked around the room. "Someone like to interview the cheerleaders and write about their view?"

Moose O'Brien, who can sleep on his feet through "The Star-Spangled Banner," sat up straighter and got an interested gleam in his eye. "Sure. I'll do that," he said.

Renee Weidt, his girl friend, came alive then too. "And I'll interview the guys on the teams. See what they think about the cheerleaders we have." She shot Moose a scalding look that he missed entirely.

"How about an article about the sexism involved in having girls as cheerleaders at all?" It was Barbara Stein. She's into sexism this year. Last year, in eighth grade, she was into boys, but they didn't much notice.

"Wait a minute," I said, standing up. Everybody turned to look at me. "I think doing a whole issue on cheerleaders is pretty dumb. I mean, who cares?"

Moose thrust out his lower lip. "I do," he said. "Most of those cheerleaders are"—he caught Renee's glare and hesitated—"interesting," he concluded, lamely.

I barreled on. "I mean, what are we in school for, anyway?" I had spent the entire evening coming up with an important issue for the paper to deal with, and I wasn't going to sit around while the staff decided to write about cheerleaders.

Everyone stared at me stupidly, except Ms. Perl, who seemed simply to be waiting.

"Because no one wants to hire us," Jimmy Fenwick stated with great authority. As long as I've known him, Jimmy has been wanting to quit school and get a job driving a truck. I can remember his having an argument with the third-grade teacher about how truck drivers didn't need to learn to read, nothing more than road signs, anyway, and he could already read every road sign he saw.

"Come on. Be serious," I said.

"I am serious," Jimmy sulked, and I knew he was.

"I'm serious too," Moose piped up, evidently having decided to ignore Renee. "I think the cheerleaders would make a good story."

Renee got up and moved to a chair on the other side of the room.

"We're here to learn. Right?" I asked, looking around for a response.

Bob Nordstrom groaned and went back to sketching cartoons. That's all Bob ever does, no matter what class he's in, draw cartoons. He was working on one of Ms. Perl. I could tell it was her because of the size of the . . . well . . . chest and because of the rest of the curves, too. There was no other model in the room for what he'd drawn on that piece of paper.

"I mean really," I protested. "And how many of you

think you're actually learning enough in your classes to justify the amount of time you spend in this place?"

Kate put her hand up, but I could have expected that. She figures that school is meant for learning, so that's what she concentrates on, whether she likes her teachers or not. After she had her hand up, though, she looked around the room and saw that no one else had responded. She ducked her head and smoothed her hair, letting her hand drop as if she'd only been attending to her hair all the time.

I continued. "I say we do the next issue of *The Roving Reporter* on an evaluation of the faculty around here. Conduct a student survey. See how many think the teachers at East are actually teaching them anything." I glanced over at Ms. Perl to see how my idea struck her. She was studying a chip in her nail polish, so it was hard to tell.

Dave nodded his approval. "Of course, everyone knows what we'll find out, but still . . . it would be better than the stuff we've been writing."

"Anything would be better than what we've been writing," Barbara said, and I couldn't help wondering where everyone had been with their critical judgment before Ms. Perl came.

"That's a super idea, Leslie," Dave said. "We could set up a survey, scientific style, of the students' opinions of the teachers, and we could interview some teachers too. See what they predict the survey will say . . . things like that."

I hadn't seen so much enthusiasm around that room since we'd planned our staff Hanukkah / Christmas party. "I'll write up the questions for a survey and do an article reporting on it," I volunteered.

Ms. Perl smiled then, and I felt warm from my toes to my scalp. I looked over at Kate to see what she was thinking of my idea now, and even she seemed pleased.

"Good idea, Leslie," Dave said. He turned to the rest of the staff and added, "Then we'll need someone else to interview the faculty . . . to provide a fair balance. And I think somebody should talk to Dr. Schultz."

While Dave was handing out the other assignments, I started gathering up my books, my mind spinning with ideas for my survey. The survey and the article I wrote from it would be the central focus of the whole issue!

But when the bell did ring, I didn't rush out the door right away. I stood beside my desk, messing with my books until all the other kids had left the room. Kate started to wait for me, but I signaled her to go on, and she did. I wanted to have a chance to speak to Ms. Perl alone. I didn't have anything to say exactly, but I just wanted . . . well, I suppose what I wanted was for her to notice me. She had started straightening up her desk and didn't seem aware that I was still there.

I cleared my throat but she didn't look up, so I

gathered my books and walked slowly up to her desk, sauntering like the whole thing was real casual.

I cleared my throat again, and this time she looked up, a slight frown making a crease between her eyebrows. Her eyebrows, I noticed, were perfectly arched. If she used a tweezers, she wasn't out of balance by a single hair.

"Uh," I said, ever eloquent, "I just wondered . . ."

"Yes?"

If there was a slight note of irritation in her voice, I could understand why. It had to be difficult, everything at the school being new for her. She must be exhausted by the end of the day after putting so much of herself into her teaching. I wasn't exactly sure what else she taught, but Miss Nelson used to teach several seventh-grade reading classes as well as advising the newspaper.

The rest of my words tripped over one another in my hurry to be done. "I just wondered if you had any suggestions . . . about my survey. You know, about what questions should be in it."

"Survey?" For a moment she looked blank, and I started to feel out of breath, as if I'd been running for a long time. I knew I was acting like an utter fool. But then she remembered.

"Oh . . . the survey about the faculty. No, no suggestions at all. You kids are the experts in that area. I'm the newcomer here." And she smiled so warmly that I could feel my face going red.

"Okay, then," I said, moving toward the door. "I'll have it ready for you to approve tomorrow."

She nodded and went back to arranging things on her desk and putting pencils away in the drawer. I told myself to move on, but somehow my feet behaved as though they were glued to the floor.

"Uh . . . ," I said, wanting just a scrap of something more, though I couldn't have said what it was I wanted, "uh . . . 'bye. See you tomorrow."

She looked up, smiled again, and again I could feel my face flush. I didn't know I was capable of being such an idiot.

"Good-bye, Barbara," she said.

I was too stunned to react. I just stood there, still rooted in the doorway. After a moment she looked up, that crease dividing her eyebrows again.

"Leslie," I said.

She looked confused.

"My name is Leslie Johnson."

"Oh." She smiled again, a really beautiful smile. "Sorry, Leslie. I'm still getting all the names sorted out."

"Of course," I said. I got my feet moving finally and ran through the thinning crowd to my locker.

As I ran I promised something to myself. Ms. Perl was going to know who I was, and soon. After I turned in my article, she wouldn't confuse me with Barbara or anybody else again. Not ever.

· · ·

"You almost missed the bus," Kate said accusingly when I dropped, breathless, into the seat next to her. "What did you stay after for, anyway?"

Her face was flat, without expression, but there was a hint of something in her eyes ... not quite amusement.

"I wanted to see if Ms. Perl had any suggestions about the survey," I said. "It was no big deal."

Kate nodded sharply as if to say "I'm sure it wasn't," but then she turned to gaze out of the bus window. She seemed to think the conversation was over.

"Wasn't that a beautiful sweater Ms. Perl was wearing today?" I said, fishing for a reaction that would let me know what was wrong.

"Mmm-hmmm," Kate replied, still not looking at me.

The sweater had been a deep cherry red, slightly fuzzy like angora.

"Such a pretty color," I added.

Kate made another noise that I took as agreement.

"It matched her nail polish perfectly. Did you notice that?"

Kate turned to face me at last. She sighed. "Aren't you taking this role-model business a little far, Leslie?"

I could feel my face turning as bright as Ms. Perl's sweater. "What ... what do you mean?" I stammered.

"It's just that you haven't talked about anything or anybody except Ms. Perl since we met her yesterday. Last night when I called, you talked about her and the newspaper the whole time, nothing else." Kate's expression was apologetic, but the words were tumbling from her mouth nonetheless.

"Well, what else is there going on in our lives that's so fascinating?" I demanded, my chest going tight.

"I don't know," Kate said, "but we usually find something."

"Such as the latest cat my mother has taken in? Wonderful!"

"How is Aslan, anyway?" Kate asked.

"As obnoxious as ever. He scratched me last night when I tried to pick him up."

Kate sighed again. "Never mind," she said.

I was furious by then. "Don't you go starting something and then saying *never mind* to me, Kate Connolly!" I pushed my face into hers until we were practically nose to nose.

"I'm sorry," Kate said, pulling away, but that didn't make me feel better. She always backs down when it comes to a real fight, and this time I would have preferred the fight. But then she continued, "It's just that I've never known you to have a crush before."

"A crush!" I repeated. "A *crush?*"

Kate was still looking apologetic, but her voice was even. "I don't know what else you would call it."

"Remember when you used to take Mr. Manslow's

picture to bed with you?" I said. "That's what I would call a crush."

"Along with my teddy bear . . . in the fifth grade," Kate replied, her voice still calm, reasonable, which was making me even more furious.

"And I suppose that's what you're trying to tell me—that I'm acting like a fifth grader?"

She shrugged. "If the shoe fits . . ."

That was the limit! I stood up and stomped to the front door of the bus, jouncing there for the last couple of blocks until my stop. If this was the way Kate was going to be, I could get along without her.

I had more important things to think about anyway—like the article I was going to write for Ms. Perl.

Four

"What's black and white and red all over?" Mr. DeWitt scratched his pot-belly and giggled. His shirt was coming untucked from the front of his pants, and he had chalk dust on his gray pin-striped suit jacket. The suit jacket was the same one he wore practically every day of the year, usually with pants that didn't match, always with streaks of chalk dust on it.

Nobody answered, not even the brownnosers, because they knew that Mr. DeWitt liked to finish off his own jokes, however obvious, old, and dumb.

I knew the answer, though. Probably everyone did. A penguin with diaper rash.

"No, not a newspaper," he said. "I know that's what you're all thinking. It's a sunburned zebra." His giggle turned higher-pitched and more intense.

The brownnosers laughed politely. The rest of us couldn't even get up the energy to groan. Mr. DeWitt looked pleased with himself. You can always tell when he's pleased, because his jowls wobble.

I went back to the survey questionnaire I was working on.

What are the characteristics that make a good teacher?

What makes a bad teacher?

What percentage of the teachers you have this year would you classify as good?

What percentage of your teachers would you say grade fairly?

Describe any unfair grading practices you know about.

Do you think teachers should waste students' time telling jokes?

I paused over that one and smiled. That would nail Mr. DeWitt for sure.

Do you think tenure should protect older teachers while younger teachers are laid off?

Mr. DeWitt was putting an algebra problem on the board. He had written $6a \times 7b = 42a$.

Practically everybody in the class saw the mistake at the same time, and kids' hands were waving all over the place.

Mr. DeWitt looked around the class in wonder the way he always does when he has done something wrong. I am sure that Dr. Schultz would be amazed at how often this tenured teacher of his makes dumb mistakes like that on the board.

"Yes, Marcie?" Mr. DeWitt said, calling on a girl who was bouncing up and down in her seat. "Was there something you wanted to say?" His face was smooth and bare of anything remotely like intelligence.

"That's wrong," she announced, triumphant.

"What's wrong?" He turned around and studied the board, his forehead wrinkled.

"The *a* in the answer." Marcie is not exactly one of the top students, but even she put on her most patient voice, as if she were talking to a little kid.

Mr. DeWitt looked at the board, still puzzled, then turned back to Marcie. "You show me, would you?" He held his chalk out to her.

Idiot! I thought, shaking my head, and I wrote another item on my survey questionnaire.

Should students be given the chance to grade teachers at the end of every course?

Marcie had written *42ab* for the answer and gone back to her seat, a look of satisfaction on her face. I gazed around the room for a moment. Mr. DeWitt had called someone from the class up to do another problem on the board. It was safer that way. He couldn't make any more mistakes.

Watching him standing there, though, I came up with my final question.

Has what you have learned from your teachers in junior high school made your time here worthwhile?

That seemed like enough. I put the sheet into my notebook and was reaching for my algebra book when Mr. DeWitt said, beaming at me the way he always did to everybody, "Leslie, what answer did you get?"

I gave him a sour look, which I'd done as a matter of principle ever since he said, "I like students who smile, and students I like are apt to get good grades." To go along with my look, I asked politely (it's all right to irritate teachers, but you have to be subtle about it), "Excuse me, Mr. DeWitt, but what problem were we on again?"

He shook his head, smiling dolefully, cutting his eyes at the class to make sure they were watching his performance. "Leslie, would you come up here, please?" He pointed to a spot on the floor right next to where he stood.

"Up there?" I asked, as if I might not have heard right. I knew, though, exactly what he had said and what it was he was going to do. Mr. DeWitt was about to go into his favorite performance.

He nodded, still smiling, still pointing at the exact place on the floor where I was commanded to stand.

I could feel my cheeks burning, and a weight seemed to have dropped through the bottom of my stomach. I glanced over at Kate, who sat across the aisle from me in algebra class, but she was staring at her algebra book as though it were the most fascinating thing in the world.

Slowly, I stood up and made my way to the front of the room. An expectant snicker ran through the class. As much as the kids disliked Mr. DeWitt, they were always willing to go along with the humorous little dramas he liked to stage. Up until now, however, I had never been the victim of one of them.

"Yes, sir," I said, when I was standing next to him. I hoped I would get off easy by being extra polite.

"Yes, sir?" he repeated. "Yes, sir! Did you hear that, class? Did you see what a polite young woman Leslie is? Exactly the kind of student I like to have in my class."

Kids were squirming in their seats, delighted with the spectacle. They reminded me of sharks, ravenous at the smell of blood. No matter that the blood came from one of their own. Only Kate was silent and solemn, but that probably wasn't out of any feeling of loyalty to me. Kate never responded to any of Mr. DeWitt's little games.

I made a silent vow that the next time Dim Wit picked on somebody I wasn't going to reward him with a single, solitary giggle, and I kept my face locked as if I didn't care. The worst thing you could do with Mr. DeWitt was to reveal that he had gotten to you, because then he would pat your arm and apologize until you wanted to throw up.

One girl had broken down and cried when he had her on display in front of the class, and for a month afterwards he walked up to her desk in the middle of class every day and asked her, quite seriously, if she was all right now. You could tell that she wanted to die all over again every time he spoke to her.

Mr. DeWitt continued with his performance. "Leslie Johnson is an excellent young woman. I know that to be true. But there seems to be one problem. Do you know what it is, class?"

"She's forgotten what her algebra book looks like," several people chorused at once, having been through this little scenario many times.

Mr. DeWitt nodded. "Kate Connolly," he said, turning suddenly to Kate whose head jerked up, her eyes widening with apprehension, "would you help Leslie, please?"

Kate stood up slowly, her face pale.

"Would you bring Leslie her algebra book?" Mr. DeWitt said.

Kate's hand snaked out to take my book off my desk, and she never looked at me once as she walked to the front of the room.

"Now, Kate," Mr. DeWitt said, sucking in his belly and tugging his trousers up, "tell Leslie what that is you have in your hand."

Kate knew the script, too, so she said, "Your algebra book," but her voice was so low that I, standing right next to her, could barely hear.

"Louder, please," Mr. DeWitt ordered, raising his hands as though preparing to direct an orchestra.

"Your algebra book," Kate repeated, a little louder, still not looking at me.

"Excellent!" Mr. DeWitt was glowing in response to the light giggle that ran beneath the surface of the class. "And can you show Leslie what page we are on, please?"

Kate fumbled through the book, her hands trembling slightly. When she found the place and held the book out to me, I took it mechanically.

"And now, Kate," Mr. DeWitt said, "show Leslie which problem we are on."

"Number five," Kate said softly, pointing and withdrawing her finger as quickly as it touched the place on the page.

"Thank you, young woman," Mr. DeWitt said, bowing slightly to Kate. "You may return to your seat now."

I watched Kate's progress back to her seat. I wanted to hurl the algebra book after her. I wanted to swear at Mr. DeWitt.

"And now, Leslie," Mr. DeWitt bent over slightly in order to beam into my face, "would you be so kind as to do problem five on page 43 for us . . . out loud, now that you have joined the class?"

Mr. DeWitt waited, still slightly bent over so he could watch my face, the air whistling in and out of his nose.

I began to read. "If a car is traveling at fifty-three miles per hour . . ."

But all the while I was reading, I was thinking, *Just you wait, Dim Wit. You're going to get yours. Through the miracle of journalism, you're going to get everything that you have coming.*

• • •

The wind blew me down the sidewalk, up the steps, and smack into the front door before I could get it opened. Brisk autumn was at an end, and icy winter was settling in, not exactly a tourist attraction in Minnesota.

When people are trying to lure tourists here for the winter, they always show a picture of a cross-country skier gliding along on a windless sunny day. You can tell even in a photo that there's no wind because the trees are standing up straight and the skier actually has his eyes open. The picture is probably taken someplace with a gentler winter, too, like Antarctica.

I backed off from the door—bright blue because my father painted the trim on our house when I was ten and blue was my favorite color—and glanced down the street at Kate's retreating back. She had waited outside the door for me after algebra class, but I walked right on by as though I didn't see her.

A real friend would have refused to help in that silly charade.

"Get down," I yelled at the mass of furry flesh assaulting me when I came in through the door. "Down!" Every day all three dogs greet me as though I've been gone for a million years. It seems to be the highlight of their day, people coming home. They go through the whole ritual again for my father when he gets home and for Brian, who plays basketball and comes home on a later activity bus.

I headed for the stairs and my room, but was stopped on the way by a sight even stranger than what I'm accustomed to at home. It was my mother, sitting in the bathtub, fully dressed—if you can call the flowered muumuu she was wearing an article of dress—holding Aslan down with one hand and spooning honey in the general direction of his mouth with the other.

"What on earth are you doing?" I asked, peering through the bathroom door. Aslan's ears were flattened to his head, and his eyes were slits of blue menace. A whining rumble that had no resemblance to a purr came from his throat.

My mother answered from between clenched teeth, grimly intent on the sticky stuff stringing from the spoon and gathering in Aslan's fur around his mouth. His teeth seemed to be clamped shut as tightly as hers. "He's still not eating. The vet said honey would keep his blood sugar up. Also, it'll make him thirsty, so he'll drink the water he needs."

"But why are you in the bathtub?" I asked, not sure I wanted to know.

Just then Aslan got a paw free enough to rake my mother's arm with his claws. She released him with a little "Oh!" and he shook his head violently, sending droplets of honey onto the sides of the tub and onto the front of my mother.

"That's why," she said, relaxed now as she watched the cat streak between my feet and disappear around the corner, pursued by all three dogs. (They wouldn't catch him. They had already done that once and learned their lesson.)

My mother unfolded her long legs and stepped out

of the tub, honey glimmering in her hair and dripping down the front of her dress. "I figure if I get enough on his fur, he'll have to lick it off. There has to be more than one way to get honey into a cat."

I shook my head. "You're a mess," I told her.

My mother laughed, turned the faucet on and dipped her hands into the running water. "Not unusual, I'm afraid."

"The climax of a wonderful day," I said, leaning against the doorframe.

I should have known better than to say something like that, because my mother's expression immediately changed to one of concern and she said, "Leslie, is something wrong?"

I turned away as if I wasn't going to answer her, but then I answered anyway. "My algebra teacher humiliated me in front of the entire class," I told her. "That's all."

Mom frowned thoughtfully, first at me and then into the mirror as she poked at a glob of honey in her hair. "Your algebra teacher? Mr. DeWitt? I'm sure he didn't mean to humiliate you."

"Not only did he mean it," I answered, crossly, "but he does it all the time. Never to me before, but to other kids. He's going to be sorry for picking on me, though."

She was back to studying me again. "What did he do?"

I shrugged. The whole thing had been awful when it was going on, but I knew it wouldn't seem like much when I tried to tell about it. "I was working on a survey for the school paper—on the students' opinion of the faculty—during class. Mr. DeWitt called on me, and just because I didn't have my book open, just because I didn't know exactly what problem we were on, he made me come up and stand in front of the class, made a whole big deal out of it. He even had Kate present my book to me, as if I didn't know what it looked like."

Mother was looking sympathetic, more sympathetic than I wanted, actually. I guess I'm hard to please sometimes. But everything I get from her is either too much or too little. The problem is, I never know which it's going to be.

"I really hate him," I said. "He's the dumbest teacher I've ever been around."

Instead of saying something soothing, which I wouldn't have minded as long as she didn't overdo it, Mother reached out and put a hand on my shoulder.

I pulled away. I couldn't help it. Her touching me like that made me feel little, almost as if I might want to cry. She let her hand drop without comment.

"Never mind," I said, "I'm going to get back at him when I do my article for the school paper."

My mother was studying me intently. "You have a new adviser for the paper, don't you?"

"How did you know?" I asked, surprised. I don't

know why I hadn't mentioned Ms. Perl at home, but I hadn't.

"Brian's in her reading class. He said she was pretty special. She used to be a reporter for the *Chicago News*, right?"

"Right," I said.

Mother started to clean out the bathroom sink, which indicated she was thinking. My mother never cleans unless she has something else on her mind. "Would you object if I looked at your survey, Leslie?" she asked.

I wasn't exactly thrilled with the idea, and I wasn't especially interested in my mother's opinion of what I was going to do. Ms. Perl had approved the survey, and that was all that mattered. It's hard to say no to a parent without seeming rude, though, so I riffled through my notebook, found the scratch copy of the page I had turned in to Ms. Perl, and handed it over.

Mom read through it quickly, went back and read it again more slowly.

"This question, Leslie," she said finally, holding the paper toward me.

"Which one?" I asked, snatching the paper from her hand.

"'Do you think teachers should waste the students' time telling jokes?'" She was reading upside down now.

"So? What about it?" I demanded. My patience

was running out.

"Isn't that," she hesitated, "unscientific, to have a survey question which dictates the answer you want? Who would say anything but no after you use a negative phrase like 'waste students' time'?"

Since when, I wondered, has my mother been so worried about things being scientific? I put the survey away. "Who cares?" I said. "I'm not a scientist. I'm a reporter, and I'm going to write an article that will show Dim Wit up for the boob he really is."

My mother was shaking her head.

"Don't be such a bleeding heart," I told her. "It's not your responsibility to protect every drowning cat and incompetent algebra teacher in Minnesota, is it?"

But she didn't say anything. She just picked up a tube of toothpaste, practically new, unscrewed the cap, and began squeezing the tube. She didn't say a word, just stood there, squeezing this long worm of toothpaste into the sink. She held the thing upside down and kept pressing, and the toothpaste kept oozing out, coiling into a pale green pile where it landed.

"Hey," I said. "Watch what you're doing!" But she ignored me. She just stood there, squeezing.

"Mother!"

She stopped then, turned, and held the half-empty tube out as if for me to take.

"What do you want me to do with that?" I asked, stepping back, staring at the lump of toothpaste at the bottom of the sink. I was certain my mother had gone over the edge at last.

Her face was solemn and her voice reasonable, though. "I want you to put the toothpaste back into the tube," she said. It might have been a perfectly rational request.

"Put it back!" I echoed. "What are you talking about? Nobody can do that!"

My mother nodded, capped the tube and set it down at last. "It's the same with words, Leslie," she said. "Once they're out of your mouth, once they're in print, you can never take them back again." She turned on the faucet, and I watched the glob of green toothpaste slide down the drain.

"Well, I promise you," I said, turning to go to my room, "I won't want to take back a single thing I write about that man."

Five

The next day we all stood outside of the classrooms between periods, handing out the surveys in clumps so they could be distributed. Before my algebra class, I stood by Mr. DeWitt's door, putting a survey into each hand that passed. When a particularly pudgy and hairy hand appeared, I looked up to see Mr. DeWitt himself, standing in front of me.

"What is this?" he asked, still holding out his hand, because I was clutching the stack of surveys against my chest. "I've been seeing them around all day. Is it a plot to overthrow the government?"

"It's a survey," I said, a bit sullenly, "for *The Roving Reporter.*"

"How interesting. I hadn't realized you were on the staff, Leslie. May I see one, please?"

"They're only for students," I said. "I mean, it's a student survey. We are," I hastened to add, "interviewing teachers more individually."

The hand didn't go away. "That sounds commendable. Still, I'm sure you wouldn't object to my seeing the survey, would you?"

I did, of course. I was afraid he would see himself in the questions, especially the one about jokes— maybe the one about tenure, too. But I handed him a copy; what else could I do?

He stood there, reading the page very slowly. My knees were beginning to feel a bit loose and wobbly by the time he handed it back. He smiled and said, so sincerely that I had to clamp my teeth to keep my jaw from dropping open, "I think this is an excellent idea. The students should have more say in the way they are taught."

He even gave everyone in the class ten minutes to fill the survey out, after regaling us with his first joke of the period. ("What do you get when you cross a tree with a box? Square roots.") He was going to collect the surveys too, but I jumped up and said, "Thanks, but I'll do it. They're supposed to be anonymous . . . sir."

Somebody in the back of the room tittered, and Mr. DeWitt stood, alternately beaming and pulling up his trousers, while I collected the surveys.

Fuel for my fire, I told myself as I gathered them up. And I felt so good that I even smiled sweetly at Mr. DeWitt.

· · ·

We sat around a table in the staff room, sorting the surveys into stacks, figuring out ways to make statistics out of the results. Ms. Perl sat with us, doing the same work we were, talking, laughing, asking us about various teachers whose names were mentioned, especially the ones the kids said were bad.

She laughed until there were tears in her eyes when I stood up and did an imitation of Mr. DeWitt.

"What do you never ask a leper for?" I asked, and then I answered myself, "A hand."

I giggled and checked everybody out to see whether or not they were laughing and vibrated my jowls all at the same time. It's a little difficult to vibrate something that you don't have, but I puffed out my cheeks, and I think Ms. Perl got the picture. Anyway, she laughed hard enough.

After I sat down again I almost felt a bit embarrassed, as if maybe I had gone too far. I wondered if Ms. Perl was going to be annoyed, but she wasn't. I've been around teachers who do things that way. They pretend to be one of the kids until something happens they don't like. Then they suddenly turn back into teachers and come down hard. Ms. Perl wasn't like that, though.

"Eighty-two percent of the kids think they don't learn enough in junior high to justify the time spent here," Dave said, looking up from the numbers he had been working with.

"Wow!" Kate said. "That many?"

"It figures," Ms. Perl commented, nodding her head.

"This is some survey, Leslie," Dave added. "I'm glad you had the idea. The information you're getting will make a terrific article."

I could feel myself blushing. Dave isn't exactly the kind to go around handing out praise casually. "Do you think it's scientific enough?" I asked. "The way I phrased the questions, I mean?"

"Sure," Dave answered. "I think it's very scientific. Don't you, Ms. Perl?"

"Of course it is," she answered. "Why do you ask?"

"Oh, it was just something my mother said."

"Your mother?" She sounded surprised that I had a mother . . . or that I would be listening to anything she said if I did.

"Well . . ." I was beginning to wonder if maybe I should have kept my mouth shut. I didn't want to go putting bad ideas about my survey into Ms. Perl's head. "The question about teachers taking class time for jokes, you know? My mother said that one was *leading,* that no one would answer anything except no."

Ms. Perl picked up a survey to read the offending question, but after she had read it, she didn't say anything more.

"I wonder how they did answer it," Dave said, beginning to leaf through the sheets of paper in front of him.

Kate started to do the same. "I can't find anything but *no* answers on my questionnaires for that one," she said. She kept her voice carefully neutral, as though what she was saying weren't anything against me . . . but I knew better.

"Your mother might have been right," Dave admitted, frowning. "All the ones I have say no to question six, too. And—"

Ms. Perl jerked the stack of papers Dave had been checking toward herself and flipped through them. "Just because most of the kids said no doesn't mean there's anything wrong with your question, Leslie. The kids are the ones who understand the situation, after all." She pushed the stack back toward Dave and smiled in my direction. "The kind of teacher you describe gives the entire teaching profession a bad name. Those people need to have a mirror held up now and then."

Dave nodded, obviously revising his opinion, but Kate still looked unconvinced.

Ms. Perl reached across the table and patted my hand. "Mothers don't know everything," she said, and she winked as though her statement were some kind of secret, just between the two of us.

"Believe me," I answered. "I know."

"The problem with parents," Ms. Perl announced to the entire room, "is that they're afraid to trust their own kids' judgment. When it comes to some things, kids are a lot smarter than most adults, but we adults don't want to admit it."

Moose cheered, and Ms. Perl nodded in his direction as though taking a small bow.

"Will you be able to have your article finished by

tomorrow, Leslie?" Dave asked. "Everything has to go to the printer's right after school."

"Sure," I said. "I'll do it tonight."

"Good," Ms. Perl said, "and I want you to have a byline on it." She turned to Barbara, who had been assigned to interview the faculty, and added, "Your article should have one, too. This will be an important campaign we're beginning, and I want you girls to get credit for your part in it."

Barbara just smiled, but I was overtaken by a sudden sinking feeling. "A byline?" I repeated. "Are you sure that's a good idea?" How many teachers would be mad at me when the next issue came out on Friday? After all, the surveys didn't exactly recommend the quality of the teaching at our school, and it occurred to me that kids can sometimes be . . . well, critical.

"A good journalist stands behind her own work," Ms. Perl said emphatically, in a tone that was almost reproving.

"Of course," I said. "I didn't mean—"

"I expect my reporters to be willing to take risks and to live up to the consequences of the risks they take," Ms. Perl went on. She spoke as though she were addressing the entire room, but I knew I was the one she was talking to. Barbara was still looking smug.

"I'll bet you stood up for your convictions when you were writing for the *Chicago News,*" Barbara said, wanting to make me look bad in contrast, I'm sure. She's that way sometimes. One day she's your friend, and the next she's not, for no reason you can ever figure out.

Ms. Perl nodded, a bit abruptly. "I was only a reporter," she said, "but I managed to take on a few controversial topics."

"What kinds of things did you report?" Dave asked. "Did you do crime in the streets and corruption in city hall . . . things like that?"

Ms. Perl's mouth quirked into a funny smile, as if there was something more amusing than what she was going to tell. "I did crime and corruption sometimes," she admitted.

"What kind of crime?" Moose O'Brien asked, sitting up straight and coming unwrapped from Renee. The two of them had been off in a corner of the room, concentrating on each other as usual.

Again that small tight smile. Ms. Perl studied her fingernail polish. It was flawless as far as I could tell. "Corruption among the higher-ups on the newspaper staff for one," she said.

"Wait a minute." Dave leaned forward, propping his elbows on his knees. His hair was blue that day, and it was standing at attention, as usual. "You mean you reported on wrongdoings on your own newspaper? You wrote articles on it and had them published . . . in the *Chicago News*? How did you get by with that?"

Ms. Perl looked up from her study of her nails. Her face was serious now. "The editor-in-chief was taking bribes from the party machine in Chicago . . . to influence the editorial policy, you know. A newspaper can have a lot of power in an election. They endorse candidates in their editorials, suggest how people should vote."

"And the party machine was paying the editor to say what they wanted him to?" Dave asked. His eyes were as wide and horrified as a little kid's who has just been told the tooth fairy died. "That's interference with the freedom of the press."

Ms. Perl nodded. "But worse than that. It's dishonest journalism. It's the press abusing its own power. Any opinions expressed on the editorial page should at least be come by honestly . . . independently."

Kate leaned forward and whispered to me, "But how did she get her editor to print articles about what he was doing?" It was the first thing she had said to me in three days, and you might figure it would be something critical of Ms. Perl.

Ms. Perl heard, and she nodded solemnly in Kate's direction. "That was the question," she said. "It was the question exactly. How could I expose corruption in our own ranks and get by with it?"

"How did you?" I asked, getting into the swing of her story. I was sure she had found a way.

Several others repeated, "Yeah. How?"

"I wrote a series of articles," Ms. Perl explained. She straightened and stacked the papers we had been working with as she talked, as though what was in front of her was a lot more important than what she was saying. But still she went on talking. "The articles were about corruption in the city in general. I exposed a connection between a paving company and the commissioner of city streets, between prostitution and the chief of police. I even uncovered a connection between a congressman's office and the biggest ring of dope pushers who'd ever operated out of Chicago."

"And wrote about it for the paper?" Jimmy asked. "Weren't you afraid somebody would come after you?"

Ms. Perl looked up for the first time, her chin held high. She looked brave and somehow frail at the same time, one woman against the entire city of Chicago. "I couldn't help being afraid . . . a little, but I knew it was what I had to do," she said.

I understood if nobody else did. "Sometimes a reporter has to be willing to take the consequences of telling the truth, doesn't she?" I asked.

Ms. Perl nodded emphatically. "That's it exactly," she answered, and she smiled at me, apparently glad someone understood.

"But why did *you* have to do it?" Sharon Simms asked.

"Why not leave it to somebody else?" Ms. Perl lifted one eyebrow in a way that said more than all her words. "Is that what you mean?"

Sharon nodded, and I was glad I hadn't told Ms. Perl I didn't want a byline. What difference did it make in the long run if Mr. DeWitt was mad at me?

Sometimes speaking the truth was more important than what happened to the one speaking.

"I don't know why I didn't let somebody else take care of it," Ms. Perl admitted, and then she smoothed her hair with the flat of her hand, and added, almost as if it were an apology, "I'm not made that way, I guess. Somebody told me once that I must have been born to cause trouble."

"And did you?" Kate was so caught up in Ms. Perl's story that she spoke out loud this time. "Cause trouble, I mean."

Ms. Perl laughed, a deep, throaty chuckle. "Gobs," she said. "Oodles. Tons. More trouble than I'd ever dreamed of."

"But what about the article about your own editor?" Dave sat forward in his chair. "About him taking bribes from the party machine to say the right things in his editorials?"

Ms. Perl looked at Dave silently for a moment, and I discovered that I was holding my breath, waiting for her to answer. What *had* her editor done? When she finally spoke, her voice was so low that we all had to strain forward to hear. Moose even unwrapped himself the rest of the way from Renee, leaving her blinking as though someone had just turned on a light. He came out of the corner, moving toward Ms. Perl's desk.

"I saved it for last, of course. I knew I'd never write anything more for the *Chicago News* after I'd turned in that article."

"You mean they fired you?" Jimmy asked, rising from his chair. "But that's not fair."

"Of course it wasn't fair." Ms. Perl shrugged as if the whole thing weren't very important anymore. "But fair doesn't have much to do with what happens to us in this world, does it?"

"Still you wrote the story," I said. "And they published it?"

She nodded. "I turned it in when I knew the editor-in-chief was out of town . . . off fishing with some of his *cronies*." She said the word as if it were something dirty, and I suppose in this case it was.

"But there would have been an assistant editor of some kind," Bob Nordstrom interjected, his voice doubtful. "Someone else would have had to approve the story."

Kate nodded.

From the sharp look Ms. Perl threw in Bob's direction, I was glad I wasn't Bob.

"I slipped the story through," Ms. Perl said. "There are ways." Her lips were pressed into a tight line as though the question had irritated her. "But then, of course, the editor came back." She sighed, gave a short, sharp laugh, then glanced around the room. She seemed to be surprised to find us still there. "He was a little man," she added, "and he had a scraggly fringe of whiskers that make his face look like a moon. His forehead turned so purple when he was yelling at me that I thought he would pop a blood vessel right then."

"Did he fire you?" It was Renee. Left on her own, she had decided, finally, to come and listen.

Ms. Perl nodded her head and sighed. "He's still there . . . running the paper." She smiled at all of us then. "And I'm here."

"I'm sorry," I said. "I mean I'm glad for us—your being here is the best thing that ever happepned to us, but I'm sorry that you got fired."

Ms. Perl shrugged and lifted her chin as though being fired were nothing, as though there weren't anything that could get her down. "Don't worry about it," she said. "It's not so bad . . . being here."

"Bad!" Jimmy said. "It's terrible. Coming to this school every day is a form of torture."

Several of the kids laughed then, and people began to mill around, gathering their books, waiting for the bell to ring. But I stayed where I was, sitting at the table with Ms. Perl.

"Thanks," I said softly, when no one else was near. "Thanks for telling us what happened to you. Now I understand, and I won't be afraid to stand behind what I write . . . no matter what happens."

Six

"What do you get when you cross a clam with an owl?"

No, not a muscle that stays awake all night, which is what you might think. You get a teacher who wastes the students' valuable time on jokes.

One teacher in particular is noted for such time-wasters and, even worse, for humiliating students in order to get a laugh from the class. That same teacher is so unfit for his job that he can't put work up on the board without making mistakes. Then, even when the mistakes are pointed out to him, he has to have a student correct them, because he still doesn't understand. Yet this teacher, and others like him, is protected by the teachers' tenure law and will continue to teach, if that is what it can be called, until he is sixty-five or chooses to retire.

So my article for *The Roving Reporter* began. I wrote it that evening and sat reading it over again and again. If I was going to get hung for what I had written, I at least wanted to make sure I was hung for something I could be proud of.

I thought about what my mother had said, about not being able to take words back once they were out, but then I remembered how it felt, being made fun of, and I wasn't sure what I had written was strong enough. Besides, I reminded myself, Ms. Perl had the courage to tell the truth about bigger issues than the incompetency of a junior high math teacher. And if Mr. DeWitt or the administration tried to do anything to me, expel me, for instance, I could get the Civil Liberties Union to defend me. A freedom-of-the-press issue would be right up their alley.

Still, I asked my mother to run me to school a little early so I would have a chance to show the article to Ms. Perl before school began.

"You've finished your article?" she asked as she pulled out of the garage. All three dogs were in the backseat, panting doggy breath all over the car. Every time my mother gets into the car, they think they have to go too, and, as often as not, she lets them.

One of them, a huge yellow mongrel named Butterscotch—my father, who loves to eat, named that one—laid his chin on the headrest of my seat and drooled on my shoulder.

"Yes," I answered, checking my notebook to see that no small corner of my article stuck out. Sometimes I suspect my mother of having X-ray eyes. "I'm taking it in to have Ms. Perl check it before school. Then if she thinks something should be changed, I can rewrite it during the day."

My mother nodded her approval. "That's a good idea, Leslie, especially when you're writing on such a controversial topic. You wouldn't want to get your new teacher in trouble with the administration, after all."

"Don't worry about Ms. Perl," I said, feeling smug. "She can take care of herself."

My mother smiled and patted Butterscotch, who had stepped over the other two dogs and was now drooling on *her* shoulder. "Still," she said, "a little care never hurts any of us."

"Of course not," I murmured, but I wasn't really listening to my mother any longer. I was thinking about seeing Ms. Perl.

When I arrived in the staff room, I found her sitting at her desk, between two huge piles of papers that must have come from her seventh-grade reading classes, recording grades in a book.

"Hi," I said, drawing in a deep breath. I don't know why it was, but there was something that made me feel breathless and a little flustered every time I tried to talk to Ms. Perl. "That looks like a lot of work. Did you have to read all those papers?"

She looked up, checked out who I was, and went back to recording grades. "Yes," she agreed, "it's a lot of work."

I could feel the heat rising to my face. What a dumb question. "Did you have to read all those papers?" Ms. Perl must have thought it was dumb too, because she hadn't answered me, really. "You know," I said, wanting to redeem myself, "If you ever need any help, I would be glad . . ."

Again she lifted her chin, looked straight into my eyes. "That's kind of you, Leslie. It really is. But I wouldn't want to take advantage—"

"It wouldn't be taking advantage," I rushed in to assure her before she could complete her sentence. "I would love doing it. I've thought I might like to be a teacher someday—unless I'm a reporter, that is—and helping you with papers would give me practice. I could see whether I liked it or not."

I was surprised to hear myself say that—about wanting to be a teacher. I've helped my dad grade papers for his fifth graders for years, and if I ever needed any convincing not to be a teacher, that had done it. Still, a person has a right to change her mind.

"Nobody likes this kind of paperwork," Ms. Perl replied emphatically, scowling at another student's name and writing a grade in her book. "You don't decide to teach because you want to grade tests."

She might have reached across her desk and slapped me. My face was purple, I could tell, because I could feel the oven that had turned on in my cheeks. Didn't she know I was just trying to start a conversation? But of course she was busy, too busy to have time for chitchat with me about what I was going to do in ten years or so.

"Uh," I said—I'm most eloquent when I'm embarrassed—"I came about my article for *The Roving Reporter.*"

"Yes?" she said, but she continued recording grades.

"I was hoping you would have time to read it."

"Sure." She kind of pointed with her chin toward a bare spot on her desk. "Just leave it. I'll look at it sometime before seventh hour."

Articulate to the core, I repeated "Uh," and this time Ms. Perl looked up, that familiar crease between her eyebrows.

"Is there something wrong?" Her voice wasn't really impatient . . . just . . . well, maybe it was a little impatient, but I could understand. After all, she had all that work to do.

"It's just that I was hoping you would have time to look at it now. Then if there are any problems, I can work on them during the day. I don't want to hold up the deadline or anything like that."

She sighed, the air hissing through tight lips, but then she almost smiled and I felt a little better. "You take your responsibilities very seriously, don't you?" she asked, and she held out one hand.

At first I didn't know what she wanted; then I realized she was reaching for my article. I wasn't sure, either, whether taking my responsibilities very seriously was supposed to be good or bad, since Ms. Perl didn't look exactly ecstatic. Still, I handed her the article and stood waiting while she flipped through the pages. She read so quickly that I was amazed. I wouldn't mind being able to read that fast.

While I went alternately hot and cold, wondering whether she was annoyed with me or not, I began scanning the upside-down names in her grade book. Halfway down the page, I came to a name that made me stop to read it again.

Brian Johnson. Of course, Mom had said Brian was in Ms. Perl's reading class, but I hadn't thought about it before, except to hope that Ms. Perl wouldn't connect him with me. Unless he said something about me, there wasn't too much chance she would. In Minnesota, Scandinavian names like Johnson are as common as snow.

Seeing Brian's name made me curious, and I checked across the page for his grades. As I could have guessed, they seesawed, each A followed by a D or an F. Brian is the kind of kid who works his heart out one minute and sloughs off the next, a perfect style for driving teachers crazy. They hate it when they can't peg you in one grade slot or another. His last grade was a D, but apparently Ms. Perl hadn't recorded his most recent grade yet. I looked at the next paper on the stack. It was Brian's, and there were no marks on it, so it was probably pretty good.

"I think it's fine, Leslie," Ms. Perl said, handing the article back to me. "Very well written."

"Uh," I said for the third time. "What about the stuff I said about Mr. DeWitt. Is that all right?"

Ms. Perl frowned slightly, took the article again, and glanced at it. "Oh," she said, "is he the teacher you're talking about in the lead?"

I nodded.

She shrugged, handed the article back. "You don't use his name. If he wants to admit your description refers to him, that's his problem."

"You don't think what I've written is too . . . I don't know, too harsh, maybe?" You would almost think that I wanted her to tell me to rewrite the lead, but of course that wasn't what I wanted really.

She picked up Brian's paper and glanced at the first page, then at her record book. She turned the paper over onto her other stack and wrote D into her book. For an instant the skin prickled on the back of my neck. Had she graded that paper? But then she looked up at me and spoke, in a tired voice, and I pushed the thought aside.

"Leslie, there are teachers like Mr. DeWitt in every school, aging and incompetent, keeping younger, better-qualified people from getting jobs. The last school where I taught was full of them, and every time they cut back, it was one of the young, alive teachers who had to go."

"The last school where you taught?" I repeated. "I didn't know you'd taught anyplace else. Was that before you were a reporter on the *Chicago News*?"

"No . . . after," she said. "I told you I got fired from the newspaper. I went back to Wittagar, that's my hometown, for a couple of years and taught."

I was disappointed, but I didn't know why. I guess I had assumed that Ms. Perl had come directly to us from the big city, still toughened from the grind of being a reporter. Wittagar was a little one-street town about fifty miles west of Minneapolis. There wasn't anything in Wittagar as far as I knew.

"Did you get laid off there because you didn't have tenure?" I asked. I hoped Ms. Perl wouldn't think the question was impertinent, but I wanted to know everything I could about her.

She nodded sharply, and I said. "I'm glad tenure's one of the things I'm writing about, then. Maybe we can get that changed here."

She looked amused. "Don't get your hopes up. I think we'll be doing well if we can get a teacher or two to see themselves as they really are."

"Like Dim Wit," I said.

"Like Dim Wit," she echoed, and we both laughed.

I stood there, pleased with the laughter we had shared, not wanting to leave. "That paper you just looked at," I said, "how did you know it was a D? Are you a speed-reader, or had you already graded it before?"

Ms. Perl lifted her chin sharply, gave me a penetrating look. "When you have all these stacks of papers," she said, "you learn to be fast."

"Boy," I said, "you sure have learned!"

She didn't answer me, picked up another paper, and went through the same process. The grade she recorded for that one was a B, right next to the previous B.

"Did you see anything in my article you'd like me to change?" I asked. "Stylistic things, I mean?"

"Leslie"—Ms. Perl stood up, walked around her desk and grasped me by the shoulders with hands that were both strong and warm—"I think you're the best writer I have on this staff, the most fluent, the most conscientious. I wish I had about eight more like you."

"Really?" I asked, my voice coming out high.

"Really!" she said, and she squeezed my upper arms where she was holding me. "Now, you had better run off to your homeroom before you're tardy. I'll see you seventh hour."

I grinned, bobbed my head, backed up. "Okay," I said. "See you seventh hour."

As I ran down the hall heading for my homeroom, my shoulders blazed where Ms. Perl had touched me. I didn't even mind that she had sent me away. I could understand her being busy, after all, and not having time for casual chitchat.

She likes my writing, my heart sang. *And I think she likes me!*

Seven

"What's that?" Mr. DeWitt asked, pouncing on the copy of *The Roving Reporter* a girl was carrying into algebra class. It was Friday afternoon, and the newspaper had been distributed in the cafeteria during lunch. I sank into my seat in the back of the room, trying to make myself short— a ridiculous effort, I know. I had been hoping against hope that Mr. DeWitt hadn't yet seen my article. If I could get out of class before he did, he would have the whole weekend to cool down before I had to face him again.

"What do you have there?" Mr. DeWitt repeated.

"It's the newspaper," the girl replied, grinning slyly. You could tell she knew about my article. Most of the kids did. Practically everybody who had come by me in the cafeteria had made a comment of some kind, mostly mentioning Mr. DeWitt.

"Oh . . . *The Roving Reporter!*" Mr. DeWitt beamed.

"Is the survey in there? The one about the students' evaluation of the faculty?"

"Yeah, it is," the girl answered, obviously delighted to be the bearer of good news.

I wanted to cream her, though I suppose there wasn't much else she could say. Anyway, I didn't know the girl at all except for seeing her in that one class, and I knew there wasn't any reason for her to try to cover for me.

"Excellent!" Mr. DeWitt set down the eraser that he had been cleaning the board with and clapped his hands like a little child. His palms sent up small puffs of chalk dust. "May I take a look at your copy? I'm anxious to see the results."

No! I silently screamed at the girl, but of course she handed her paper over. A light titter ran through the class, reminding me of Mr. DeWitt's drama the week before.

Mr. DeWitt smiled back at the class. You would think he had just told one of his jokes and understood the laughter. He took the newspaper and began leafing through it. I slumped farther down into my seat. My article was on the front page, and my only hope was that he wouldn't see it since he had turned immediately to the inside.

"Try page 1," one of the boys called out, and I sank down until my chin was practically on my desk.

Mr. DeWitt turned back to the front page, scanned it with a puzzled look. He still didn't see my article, and I was sitting there with my toes practically crossed inside my shoes.

"Here it is!" he said suddenly. "And our own Leslie Johnson wrote it, too. Isn't that nice?"

Lovely, I thought. *Why didn't I think about a moment like this? How could I have been so dumb?* My mother had warned me, after all. Maybe that was why I couldn't let myself think of it, because my mother *had* warned me.

This time the titters surfaced for a moment and then subsided again. Mr. DeWitt jerked up his trousers and looked around with an open, foolish grin, obviously waiting to share the joke.

"Why don't you read the article, Mr. DeWitt?" one of the boys called. "Read it out loud."

"Yeah, we were too busy during lunch. We haven't had a chance to read it yet," somebody else lied.

Clarissa Miles, the class brain, added with mock solemnity, "Learning how to evaluate the people who teach us is an important part of our education," and, to my horror, Mr. DeWitt nodded his agreement.

Whose side were all these kids on, anyway? I had never done anything to any of them.

"All right," he said, "but I don't think I should read it. Leslie should be the one." He was looking at me, beaming, holding the paper out. "Leslie, you come right up here."

"The article is rather long," I protested. "We shouldn't take the time away from our algebra, should we?"

The giggles that had been bubbling to the surface of the room erupted into full-scale laughter.

Mr. DeWitt laughed, too, as though he understood the joke. "I've never known such an attack of conscientiousness in a student" he said, "and it's come on you so suddenly, too." He held out the paper for me, there at the front of the room, and for the second time, I had no choice. Slowly, my hands clammy and my legs like Jell-O, I stood and walked toward him.

The kids shifted delightedly in their seats, nudged one another, exchanged conspiratorial looks. Only Kate was perfectly still, her face tight and closed so I couldn't guess what she was feeling. She was probably laughing as much as everybody else on the inside.

The undercurrent of reaction all over the room was like a silent air-raid siren. How was it that Mr. DeWitt, after all his years of teaching, couldn't figure out that something ugly was going on? Did a person go blind and deaf standing in front of mobs of junior high students year after year?

I made one last attempt at diverting the disaster . . . or at least postponing it. "Don't you think Mr. DeWitt, that the kids would rather read it themselves . . . on their own time?"

"I think you're too modest for your own good, Leslie. I really want you to read your article. I wouldn't have asked you if I didn't."

He thrust the newspaper closer until I had to take it, then he patted my shoulder clumsily, at the same time propelling me toward the center of the room. "I've noticed in class," he added, "that you tend to hold yourself back, even when you know the work as well as anybody. Now is your moment to shine, and I insist that you shine, right here where I can see you."

My hands trembled as I took hold of the paper. I had had a few bad imaginings since I had written the article, but none had been as terrible as this. This was like those dreams you have where you're standing in front of a whole bunch of people without any clothes on.

I cleared my throat, looked helplessly at the clock; there were still forty minutes before class was over. No use hoping for rescue by the bell. I considered praying fervently for a fire alarm or some other rescue from on high, but I didn't. My father always says that prayer is not a way of magically controlling the world. Too bad.

"Go on," Mr. DeWitt said, beaming at me as though I were his star pupil instead of some jerk who sat in the back of the room and refused to laugh at his jokes.

I opened my mouth, but at first no sound came out. My tongue felt like a wad of cotton. "Don't you think—?" I asked, looking toward Mr. DeWitt, but he interrupted me.

"Read," he commanded, putting on the voice of authority.

So I read.

While I read the joke—"What do you get when you cross an owl with a clam?"—I knew, without even looking, that Mr. DeWitt was grinning at the class. He knew, of course. I was writing about him. He couldn't help but know. On Monday he had told that joke, twice in my class alone. But then I read further, about the teacher wasting the students' valuable time, and as I read, I watched Mr. DeWitt out of the corner of my eye. The grin slowly faded from his face. He stepped back like someone staggering under a blow and reached out one hand to the chalkboard behind him.

"Shall I go on," I asked, my head lowered over the paper, wishing I couldn't see his face.

"Yes, yes, of course," he said, straightening up and moving away from the board with obvious effort. "Go on reading."

And so I went on . . . to the bitter end, my words stumbling over one another in my haste to be done. When I had to turn to page 3 to complete the article, my hands were trembling so violently I could barely turn the page.

After I had read the last words, an impassioned plea for abolishing the tenure rule, for students to be given the opportunity to rank their teachers, for an education dedicated to learning instead of to parroting instructors, there was a heavy silence in the room. All the earlier laughter had died, and now the kids looked embarrassed and uncomfortable, which was worse than having them laughing, if you want to know the truth. Much worse.

I folded the paper, pretending it was the most important thing in the world, folding that paper up just the way it had been. I wanted to disappear from the face of the earth and never return again.

I tried to remind myself that I had been provoked, but the other little drama in front of the class had faded away to nothing in contrast to this. I couldn't help wondering, for just a moment, why Ms. Perl had gone along with my idea, why she hadn't warned me. Then I wondered if she'd had so much trouble herself that she didn't care about other people's troubles any more . . . especially mine.

Mostly I kept seeing, as if it were right there behind my eyelids, a glob of green toothpaste in the bottom of the bathroon sink.

"Well," Mr. DeWitt said. "Well."

But then he sputtered into silence, like a motor running out of fuel. The room was quiet for so long that I looked up to see if he was still there. He was. He hadn't moved. He was simply standing there in front of the class, and his face was the dull white of old snow . . . with a bit of a yellow tinge to it. He was wringing his hands, holding them in front of his chest and twisting them violently, and his mouth kept opening and closing as if he were trying to say something. But not a sound came out—not a single, solitary sound.

He's going to have a stroke, I thought, but then he seemed to gather himself together a bit.

He bowed slightly toward me and toward the class, said in a thin, squeezed-out voice, "Excuse me, please," and turned and tottered from the room.

Eight

After Mr. DeWitt had disappeared through the door, I returned to my seat in the back of the room, sank into it, and buried my face in my hands. I couldn't decide whether I felt like crying or like throwing up.

The buzzing excitement of the class swirled around me like wind around the eye of a hurricane, but no one spoke to me. It was as though I weren't there. Eons later when the bell rang, everyone ran for the door, leaving me sitting by myself in the back of the room.

Only Kate remained when all the others were gone. She walked over to where I was sitting and stood there without saying anything at first. When I looked up, finally, she said, "Everything you wrote was completely true."

"Thanks" I muttered, "but not exactly kind, right?"

Kate scratched at something on the edge of her algebra book. "I don't know," she said. "Maybe in journalism, kindness doesn't count for much."

I could have hugged her, but instead I gathered up my books and got up to walk with her to our lockers. There has never been a time in my life when I've needed Kate and she hasn't come through.

Rumors flew around the school during the next periods. It's amazing how free the flow of information is through an educational institution. Someone had seen Mr. DeWitt in Dr. Schultz's office, sobbing. Someone had heard he had had a heart attack and had been taken to the hospital. Someone else knew, beyond a shadow of a doubt, that after reading the article, Dr. Schultz had stomped into the faculty lounge where Mr. DeWitt had been hiding and had fired him on the spot. In evidence, Mr. DeWitt had come back to his classroom during his free fifth hour and loaded everything from his desk into two large grocery sacks and then had been seen shuffling sorrowfully out of the school.

Every time I saw Kate, she said, quietly and seriously, "Don't worry, probably none of it is true." But still, by the time I arrived at journalism class seventh hour, I was feeling pretty sick.

"Ms. Perl," I said, as I came through the door, "have you heard?"

But Ms. Perl was putting on her coat, talking to Dave as she adjusted the collar. I was the one she didn't seem to have heard.

"I'd appreciate that, Dave," she was saying, "and I'll see you on Monday."

Dave nodded vigorously, his cheeks glowing pink. It was the first time I realized he was a bit in love with Ms. Perl . . . too.

"Ms. Perl," I repeated as she gathered some papers off her desk and headed for the door, but she merely raised her hand in my direction, palm forward, as though she were a traffic cop and I was an approaching truck. For an instant the gesture made me angry, made me want to run her over, but of course I didn't. I merely dropped heavily into the nearest chair and watched her leave.

"What was that all about?" I asked Dave, who was still looking enormously pleased with himself but a bit bewildered.

"Actually," he said, "I'm not sure. She just told me she had to go home."

"Home?"

"Not home here in the city. Home to where her parents live. Witty . . . something."

"Wittagar," I said dully.

"Yeah . . . that's it. Something about her father being sick. She asked me to cover for her."

Kate had come in and was listening to our conversation. "Cover for her? Do you mean lie?"

Dave rumpled his forehead. "I don't think that's what she meant. More just take care of things, but . . . I don't know." He turned up his hands, his steel-studded wristbands sparkling in the classroom light.

"Have you heard what happened to Mr. DeWitt?" Barbara demanded, appearing in the doorway.

"What?" I asked, wondering which version of the story she had heard or if a new one was going around.

"Well, right after he read your article in *The Roving Reporter*, he just walked—"

"Where's Ms. Perl?" It was Dr. Schultz standing in the doorway, one hand clenched on the lapel of his tweed jacket as though he were holding up his thin frame. "Isn't she here?"

We all jumped, but no one answered. After an awkward silence, Dave took a step toward Dr. Schultz. "Ms. Perl had to go home," he said, "because her father is sick. She left me in charge."

Dave's hair, which was green that day and standing up like the quills on an excited porcupine, seemed to catch Dr. Schultz's notice more than his words. "Home?" he repeated, visibly collecting himself. "She went home? But she hasn't been by the office to—"

"I don't think there was time," I interrupted. "It seemed to be an emergency." And then I added, as though it were pertinent to Ms. Perl's going off in such a hurry, "Her father lives in Wittagar."

Dr. Schultz ran his fingers through his grizzled hair and scowled. "Are you Leslie Johnson?" he asked, and I swallowed hard and admitted that I was. In all my time in junior high I had managed to avoid any personal contact with Dr. Schultz, and I was surprised he knew who I was.

He looked me over, his frown deepening, then turned on his heel. "Come with me," he barked, and he stomped out of the room without checking to see whether or not I would follow. Obviously he was accustomed to being obeyed.

I looked to Dave and Kate for some kind of rescue, but of course there was nothing they could do, so I followed Dr. Schultz out of the room, down the echoing hall, and to his office.

The principal's office is carpeted and plush, with a wide, shining desk of dark wood and a padded chair, which Dr. Schultz settled into wearily. I had never been inside his office before. Like the fly in the spider's parlor, I would gladly have foregone the pleasure.

I stood, just inside the door, my hands buried in the pockets of my jeans.

"Sit down." Dr. Schultz indicated a straight-backed chair, appropriate for a victim of the Inquisition. I sat down. A copy of *The Roving Reporter* was on his desk.

"Would you like to tell me about this?" he inquired, holding the paper up.

I don't know why people in authority do that, pretend to be carrying on a friendly conversation when they are only building up steam to roll over you.

"What do you want to know?" I asked.

"Why did you write such an article, for a starter?"

I shrugged. Why had I written it? Because I'd owed Mr. DeWitt one, but I couldn't say that. "Because students have a right to consider what makes a good teacher."

"Do you also have a right, in a school-sponsored publication, to attack a member of the faculty?"

"It wasn't exactly an attack," I said. "At least, I didn't mean it to be."

Dr. Schultz snorted, his nostrils pinched. "What did you mean it to be, then?"

"The truth," I answered, and I looked him in the face for the first time.

Dr. Schultz stared back at me for a long, intensely silent minute. "The truth," he muttered, finally. "Why is it delivered only to the very young?"

I didn't understand what he meant by that, and if I had understood, I suspect he wouldn't have wanted any answer anyway, so I just waited. When Dr. Schultz didn't seem to be going to say anymore, I took a deep breath and dared, finally, to ask, "Is Mr. DeWitt all right? He isn't sick or anything, is he?"

Dr. Schultz had been leaning forward across his desk, looking like a vulture about to pounce. In response to my question, he rubbed his face and leaned back in his chair. "No, he's not sick. But no, he's not all right."

"What . . . what do you mean?"

"I mean that a man who has taught in this school

for forty-one years walked into my office today and resigned. He had two and a half years yet that he could have continued teaching, and he quit, effective today."

"He'll still get his pension, won't he?" I asked. I had heard my father talking often enough about his pension, what would and would not be possible for him and my mother when he retired. I knew that you had to teach a certain number of years—though certainly Mr. DeWitt had done that—before you could qualify.

Dr. Schultz gave me that look again, the look adults give you when they think you belong on another planet. "Yes," he barked, biting the word off. "He'll get his pension."

"Oh," I answered. I didn't know what else I was supposed to say.

Dr. Schultz didn't seem to need anything more, because he went on. "He had been dreading retirement, you know, hating the thought of it. He loved teaching."

"*Loved* teaching?" I could feel my jaw drop.

Dr. Schultz nodded grimly. "Hard to believe, isn't it? That someone who told bad jokes loved teaching."

"Oh," I said. "But it wasn't just the jokes!"

Dr. Schultz waved my words away with one hand. It was obvious he didn't want to hear what it was besides the jokes. For a moment I relived standing in front of the class, having my algebra book delivered to me, the snickers of the kids. It was a crummy way to teach; there was no doubt about that, but maybe there was something crummy about my vengeance, too.

"Well," Dr. Schultz said, standing up. "You got what you wanted. I hope it pleases you."

"No," I said, "it—" But he interrupted.

"Just two and a half more years, and he could have left with his dignity intact."

When Dr. Schultz looked at me, I almost could have sworn his eyes were moist. He shook his head, sighed. "You may go, Leslie, but *The Roving Reporter* is disbanded, as of today. Tell the staff they are to come to the office for new class schedules Monday morning."

"Disbanded!" I stood up, reeling. Never to be in Ms. Perl's class again! "You don't mean . . ."

He nodded abruptly. Obviously, he did.

"And if you happen to talk to your teacher," he said, "tell her I want to see her in my office . . . first thing Monday morning."

For an instant, relief sizzled up my spine. Dr. Schultz was going to blame Ms. Perl, not me. But that reaction was followed immediately by a rush of shame. How could I have thought such a thing? There wasn't that much the administration could do to me. I was only a kid, after all, and what did I know? The only writing I had done before this was a gossip column. I couldn't be expected to know anything, could I? But Ms. Perl—Ms. Perl was faculty, and she could be fired.

If she was, it would be entirely my fault.

Nine

I walked back toward the staff room as slowly as I could. Dr. Schultz was going to disband *The Roving Reporter*, disband the paper and probably fire Ms. Perl! Because of me.

Why hadn't I listened to my mother's lecture about toothpaste? Why hadn't Ms. Perl warned me that the article would cause trouble? Why hadn't I known for myself?

I stopped and leaned against a locker for support, feeling dizzy and sick. I had gotten everything into such a mess. I couldn't face the rest of the staff. They would never forgive me. Only Kate wouldn't care that much, because she hadn't liked the newspaper work anyway . . . and she hadn't liked Ms. Perl.

Ms. Perl. I could never face her again, if I ever had a chance to see her again. She'd only been in the job for two weeks. Dr. Schultz *could* fire her. He probably wouldn't even have to give her any notice. She certainly wasn't protected by tenure.

There had to be something I could do—something that would make a difference. I couldn't just stand by and see everything go down the drain, along with Mr. DeWitt. Why did I care about Mr. DeWitt? He had humiliated me, hadn't he? Made fun of me in front of the entire class? But already that didn't seem to matter so much anymore. Would a moment come when my article no longer mattered to Mr. DeWitt?

I pushed off from the locker where I had been leaning and started for the journalism class. At least I could try to do something, instead of sitting around and waiting for the ax to fall. There had to be some way to save everything—*The Roving Reporter* and Ms. Perl!

When I got to the staff room, everybody stopped talking as I came through the door and stared at me as though I were some kind of freak. Only Kate got up to greet me. I could see how this was going to go. My survey had been a *staff* survey up until now. Suddenly it was all mine, along with all its results.

Dave came to join Kate and me.

"What did the old man want?" he asked in a low voice.

I told them what Dr. Schultz had said, about Mr. DeWitt's resigning, about disbanding *The Roving Reporter*.

Dave clamped his mouth into a tight line. "What about Ms. Perl?" he demanded.

"I don't know for sure," I admitted, "but I think he means to fire her. He said if I talked to her to tell her he wanted to see her in his office Monday morning."

"What did you tell him?" Dave asked, suddenly angry. "I suppose you made the whole thing her fault."

"No, I didn't. I didn't say *anything* about Ms. Perl. *He* was the one who brought her up."

"And did you defend her?" he asked, crossing his arms over his chest.

I wanted to hit him, to push in his face, but instead I answered, "There was nothing to defend. Dr. Schultz knows I'm the one who wrote the article. That's what we talked about."

"Okay, okay," Dave said roughly. "Be quiet and let me think."

I was quiet, but my hand kept clenching into a fist as if it might decide to hit Dave all on its own.

He hunched his shoulders and flexed the muscles in his upper arms. (He was wearing a leather vest with a torn T-shirt underneath, but don't ask me why he hadn't been sent home to put on proper clothes. I think most of the teachers are afraid of him, if you want to know the truth.) "You've got to go see Mr. DeWitt," he said, at last, "talk him out of quitting. If he changes his mind and stays, then they can't do anything to Ms. Perl."

"Talk to Mr. DeWitt?" I gasped. "Me?"

Dave nodded. "You've gotta. It's the only way."

But Kate was shaking her head. "You didn't see what he did to Leslie, how awful he was. He deserved every word Leslie wrote."

"Who cares what he deserves?" Dave shouted. "Ms. Perl doesn't deserve to be fired!"

"Is Ms. Perl going to be fired?" Bob Nordstrom broke in from across the room. I shook my head at him, and he went back to his drawing.

"You don't understand," I said to Dave. "I couldn't go talk to Mr. DeWitt! You didn't see the look on his face after I'd finished reading that article."

"Then what are we going to do? You come up with a plan." Dave was looking as tough as possible for someone his size . . . especially with bright green hair.

I sank into the nearest chair and groaned. "I want to do something, but not that. Anything but that. I couldn't face Mr. DeWitt again. I really couldn't."

"I have an idea." It was Kate. "Why don't we talk to Ms. Perl, tell her what's happened? She could go see Mr. DeWitt, talk him out of resigning."

Dave beamed, clapped his hands like a little kid. "And if Mr. DeWitt takes back his resignation, Dr. Schultz won't be able to do anything to her—or disband the paper, either!"

"But how do we find her?" I demanded. "She's gone home to Wittagar."

"I know!" Dave raised a fist in the air. "We'll call her, right now! Wittagar's a small town. There's probably only one Perl there. We'll get her father's number from Information."

Kate and I looked at each other, nodding our heads in agreement. Dave was already out the door before we could get ourselves turned around.

"Are you running out now that you've gotten us all in trouble?" Barbara called after me as Kate and I went out the door. I ignored her and hurried into the hall, catching up to Dave at the telephone. He was arguing with Information.

"Are you sure?" he asked. "Would you check again?" He listened for a few seconds, then shook his head. "That can't be it."

He hung up the phone and turned to face us, scowling. "The operator says there is no one by the name of Perl in Wittagar. There's a Perlowski, but no Perl."

"But there has to be," I argued. "I know that's where her family lives. She told me."

"Maybe her father's number is unlisted," Kate suggested.

"Maybe," Dave agreed, then they both stood there staring at me, as though the next move were mine.

I backed up. "There's nothing I can do," I said. "Mr. DeWitt wouldn't listen to me. He wouldn't even let me in the door."

Kate nodded glumly at Dave.

"Okay," he said. "then let's go to Wittagar and talk to Ms. Perl, all of us. It's not very far, and she can't be hard to find in a town that small."

"Go to Wittagar? How would we get there?" I asked. "Are you stealing cars these days?"

Dave grinned as though the idea of stealing cars rather appealed to him, but he said merely, "I can get us there. Don't worry."

"And back?" Kate demanded.

"Sure. Ms. Perl will bring us back when she comes to see Mr. DeWitt."

"But what if she doesn't want to do that? I mean, what if she doesn't want to see Mr. DeWitt at all?" I was feeling as if the floor I was standing on had just turned into a conveyor belt without any warning.

Dave looked disgusted. "Why wouldn't she? It's her job we're trying to save."

Even Kate agreed. "It only makes sense," she said.

"What will we tell our parents?" I asked next. "I don't know about you, but I'm not in the habit of running off without telling anyone, and mine would never agree to let me go."

Dave shrugged. His shrug made me wonder if he even had parents, but always obedient Kate said, "I'll call my mother and tell her I'm going home with you. You can call yours, and say you're going to my house."

I stared at her, astonished. "How come you're willing to help?" I asked. "You don't even like Ms. Perl!"

Kate was concentrating on a crack in the tile floor. She answered so softly that I almost didn't get her reply. "I know it's important to you," she said.

"Okay," I answered, Kate's loyalty giving me new courage, "we call our mothers."

Kate's call was easy to make. All she had to do was to leave a message with her mother's secretary.

When I called my house, I hoped against hope that my mother would be out. She wasn't.

"Uh, hi, Mom," I said, trying to remember exactly what I had meant to say. Lying just isn't my bag.

"Hi, Leslie," my mother replied. Then, her antennae apparently aquiver, "Is something wrong?"

"Why would anything be wrong?" I used that tone of instant disgust that is good in keeping parents at bay.

"I just thought you might have missed the bus or something," she answered, unperturbed.

"The bus hasn't even left yet," I said, and then I added, letting the words tumble out without any particular plan, "I thought I'd go home with Kate, probably have dinner with her. We have some studying to do."

"Studying? On Friday night?" my mother asked. I couldn't tell if she was astonished or amused.

"Why not?" I shot back. "Unless you have some objections."

"Of course I don't," she said, still sounding cheerful. "Have a good time."

"A good time?" I repeated. "Doing homework?" My words dripped sarcasm. I sounded as if I'd convinced myself that was really what I was going to do.

There was a pause at the other end of the line. I had the feeling my mother was waiting for me to say something more, to give myself away. When I didn't, she said, "Your father is helping out with Brian's basketball game tonight, but I'll be home. Call if you need a ride."

"Sure," I said. And then, "Thanks."

"By the way, Leslie." (I knew what the question would be before she had a chance to get it out.) "Isn't this the day your article was going to come out in *The Roving Reporter?*"

"Yeah," I said. "What about it?"

"I just wondered how it went."

"How could it go?" I said. "Nobody pays any attention to a school paper." *How I wished that were true!*

Just before I hung up I heard a chorus of yapping in the background followed by a long-drawn-out howl, probably Aslan drawing blood again. I slammed the receiver down and turned to Dave, demanding, "Now tell us how you're going to get us to Wittagar."

Dave was the picture of nonchalance. "We'll hitch," he said.

"Hitch!" I practically went through the ceiling. "What are you talking about?"

Kate's eyes grew round.

"Look," Dave said. "I thought you wanted to help Ms. Perl and save *The Roving Reporter* and turn things around with Mr. DeWitt."

"I do," I snapped back, "But I want to get to Wittagar in one piece."

Dave shrugged. "I hitch rides all the time. And there are three of us. What do you think anybody is going to do to three people together?"

Sometimes I feel like there must be something wrong with me. I seem to be made out of orneriness. Whatever topic is under discussion, I can be counted on to take the other side. If Kate and Dave had wanted to stay home and do nothing, I would have wanted to go to Wittagar, been the one figuring out how we were going to go.

The bell rang then, and a swarm of kids poured into the hall, surging toward us like a tidal wave.

"Okay," I said. "I'll go, but how do we find a ride?"

Dave nodded sharply, like a soldier receiving a command. "I know where to go," he said. "Just leave it to me."

· · ·

The *where to go* that Dave knew turned out to be nothing more than a Phillips 66 station on Highway 12.

While Kate and I huddled inside the gas station next to a pop machine, Dave walked casually from one car or truck that pulled up to the next, speaking to each driver briefly. He had pulled a stocking cap over his green hair, and a jacket covered his leather vest and his studded wristguards, so he looked pretty normal. Still, after speaking to each driver, he nodded, backed off, waited for the next car.

After quite a few attempts, he came to the driver of an ancient red pickup and spoke to him as he was pumping gas. Dave stayed on this time, talking, occasionally nodding in our direction. When the man turned around to look, I stood where I was, alternately smiling and sucking in my cheeks, trying to look harmless and like I wouldn't take up much space. I hoped Kate was doing the same.

The man turned back to Dave, and they talked some more. Finally the driver nodded and took the nozzle back to the pump. Dave did a little skip-hop, then sauntered in our direction.

"Come on," he said, poking his head in the door. "We're on our way."

"What did you tell that guy?" I asked.

Dave shrugged. "I told him the truth, what else? I said that my sister and I wanted to visit our grandmother in Wittagar and that our car had broken down. We have our parents' permission to make the trip, of course."

"Your sister?"

Dave grinned. "Would you rather have been my wife?"

I grimaced. "Sister will do. Thanks." And I started for the door.

"What about me?" Kate asked in a small voice.

Dave opened the door and waved her outside. "Come along, cousin. Our grandmother would be terribly disappointed if she didn't get to see you, too."

Kate shook her head, but she took a deep breath and marched gamely toward the pickup.

It was a tight squeeze. Kate sat next to the driver, putting her feet gingerly on each side of a spittoon supported by the floor hump in the middle, and Dave sat next to her. I sat on the outside. The door closed with a tentative sound, like it wasn't sure it meant to stay closed.

The driver was an older man, probably in his sixties, with a long, grayish face and a bald head that seemed to give him an extra forehead. There would have been room for a second nose and another pair of eyes, right above the first ones. He grunted something that might have been hello or might have been something entirely different. I looked at Dave. He shrugged and rolled his eyes.

"What did you say your name was?" the man asked, after we had left the suburbs behind and headed west on Highway 12. The setting sun made his face glow orange.

"Wiley," Dave answered.

Neither Kate nor I said anything. It was hard to help out when we weren't sure what Dave had already said.

The man was silent for about ten miles, and then he said, "There ain't no Wileys in Wittagar that I know of. Mostly Slavs and Poles there."

It was hard to tell if it was an accusation or a complaint.

"Wiley is our father's name, of course," Dave said

quickly. "It's our grandmother on our mother's side we're visiting."

Good old Dave, I thought.

Another ten miles passed, and I thought we were home free, but then the man said, running one hand over the top of his bald head as if the smoothness of it comforted him, "What's your grandma's name?"

I could feel Dave go rigid. He didn't answer, and Kate didn't either.

Nobody's going to say anything, I thought. *We're all going to sit here like bumps, and nobody's ever going to think of an answer.*

Grandma, I thought of saying. Her name's Grandma. But we were too old to get by with anything as dumb as that.

Then Dave squared his shoulders, and I knew everything was going to be all right. "Can't you guess?" he asked, his voice rising with his own cleverness. "Everybody says my sister favors our grandma so much that you'd know what family we were from just by looking."

The old man turned and studied my face until I looked away, hoping he would go back to watching the road. I could feel the instant he took his eyes off me, like a pressure lifted from my skin, but I kept looking out the window anyway. Nobody spoke again for a long time, but this time the silence didn't feel like safety. It felt like being hung out over a cliff by a tattered rope.

"Stella Wilensky?" the man offered finally.

Dave grinned, nudged me in the ribs, and laughed. "I knew you'd figure it out," he said. "Everybody who knows Grandma always does. It's uncanny, isn't it, how much Leslie looks like her?"

"Uncanny," the old man grunted in agreement. I tried to relax back into the seat, turning to watch the bare, harvested fields that flowed away from us on every side like a brown sea. Maybe Dave had convinced the old man, but I wasn't sure.

"Most uncanny thing I ever seen," the driver added suddenly, his words rasping like the pickup's laboring motor. He took a dark roll of chewing tobacco out of his coat pocket and gnawed off a hunk.

"Why's that, sir?" Despite his saying *sir*, Dave's words had the patronizing quality that people use talking to little children and incompetents. I leaned forward, jostling Dave's shoulder, wishing there were some way I could warn him. This old man wasn't to be fooled with. I didn't know why, but I could tell.

"Because," came the reply, a little muffled by the chew of tobacco bulging in one cheek, "there ain't no Stella Wilensky in Wittagar."

Dave's head jerked as if someone had pulled him up by the hair. "There ain't . . . I mean, there's not?" he stammered. "I don't understand. Do you suppose she's moved and nobody told us?"

The old man chuckled then, but whatever the joke

was, I knew it was on us. "Stella Wilensky is my wife," he said, "and she and me live on a farm, a ways beyond Wittagar."

Dave sank down in his seat, a slight gurgling sound coming from the back of his throat. Obviously it was time he had a little help. It wasn't his fault this fellow was so crafty.

"Okay," I said, "so that's not why we're going to Wittagar, but we appreciate the ride. We don't want you to think we don't."

Mr. Wilensky leaned over and spat a dark streak of tobacco juice in the direction of Kate's feet. If Kate could have turned into a turtle and retracted her legs, she would have, I knew, but since there was nowhere to go, she simply sat looking down at the spittoon between her feet. At least he'd hit it.

"Stella and me never had any kids," Mr. Wilensky said to nobody in particular. "Time was we used to feel pretty bad about that, but"—he eyed each of us in turn and then shook his head slowly—"not anymore. Guess when I look around, I'm grateful to have been spared the trouble."

Ten

"Maybe we should have asked him," Kate said, standing next to me in the snowy road and watching the red pickup clatter away.

"Asked him what?" I stood there, hunched inside my coat, looking around. Wittagar's main street was three blocks long. From where we stood, we could see to the edges of town, and there wasn't a soul in sight. Dry leaves rattled in the gutters. Except for a restaurant across the street, everything seemed to have closed down for the day.

"If he knew Ms. Perl. He might have been able to tell us where her house is."

"If her house is even here," I said. "Remember, the operator said there wasn't anybody named Perl in town."

"You said she told you she came from Wittagar," Dave said. "Right?"

"Right," I answered. It *was* what she had told me.

"Then she's here," he said with complete confidence.

But mine faded as we stood there on the curb, gazing around at the bleak little town.

"That restaurant over there looks open," Kate said finally.

And Dave added, "We can ask there. Everybody knows everybody in a town this size."

A chill wind swooped down the street and passed between my ribs. *What are we doing here?* I wondered as I followed Dave and Kate across the street and through the door of the restaurant. The heavy smell of frying hung in the air. *We must all be crazy.*

We stood next to the cash register for a few minutes. No one paid any attention to us except for the deer's head on the wall, which stared at us with glassy brown eyes. Obviously this wasn't the kind of place where you had to wait to be seated.

"I vote we get something to eat first," Dave said. "Then we can ask the waitress."

There were half a dozen tables filled and one waitress moving between them. The people all looked middle-aged or older, but the atmosphere wasn't like most restaurants in the cities where older people go. The diners here called back and forth between the tables in a friendly way. After a curious glance, no one paid any attention to us, though.

Kate and I followed Dave to a booth and sat staring around the room to avoid one another's eyes. I wondered why I had allowed Dave to talk me into coming here. I wondered, assuming we did find Ms. Perl, how she was going to feel when we showed up on her doorstep.

"Don't you think you ought to take off your hat?" I asked Dave in a low voice when my gaze traveled back to him.

Dave looked around, smiled, and shook his head. "I think the hair would be more of an insult than the hat," he answered.

"Why do you do that to your hair anyway?" I asked. I was feeling annoyed with Dave for having brought me to such a place, though I knew I should have been grateful that he was there with me at all.

We were all watching the waitress who was waiting on a table on the other side of the room. She was a large blond woman with dark eyebrows penciled onto a perfectly bare brow.

Dave shrugged, even blushed a little. "To bug my father, I suppose. At least it would bug him if he were around to see."

"Where is he?" Kate asked. My questions had been irritable pokes. Kate's sounded interested and sympathetic.

"He's in the marines," Dave answered. "But I haven't seen him since I was in the fifth grade. That's the year he quit coming home on his leaves."

"Don't you miss him?" Kate asked softly.

Dave shook his head. "No. I just wish he'd come home and take a good look."

"How long are you going to stay punk if your father never shows up to be shocked?" I asked. I had meant to be as sympathetic as Kate, but I sounded like a crabby teacher.

Dave grinned. "I don't know. It's a pretty good character test, actually. I can find out a lot about people by how they react to the way I look. Ms. Perl, for instance, she never batted an eye."

Ms. Perl. Something inside my chest tightened at the name. What was she going to say when I told her about the paper's being disbanded because of my article, about Dr. Schultz wanting to talk to her? Would she still say that it was important to get people like Mr. DeWitt to see themselves as they are?

I wondered, too, how much she had actually heard before she left school. Not much, I supposed, or she wouldn't have left. She had been teaching classes all afternoon—and, of course, she must have been worrying about her father—so she probably hadn't heard a thing. If she knew about Mr. DeWitt, she would have said something to me before she left. Most likely she wouldn't have left at all, unless her father's illness was a real emergency.

The waitress came to take our order. "Could you tell me," I asked, after we had ordered cheeseburgers and fries, "where Meredith Perl lives?"

"Meredith Perl?" The woman raised those neatly drawn eyebrows until they disappeared beneath her bangs. "There's nobody around here by that name that I know of."

"No one?" I repeated, weakly. Which was worse, I wondered, to have hitched fifty miles to see Ms. Perl and not be able to find her, or to have to face her with what had happened?

Dave intervened. "There has to be. Ms. Perl teaches in the Twin Cities, now, but she comes from this town. Her parents live here."

"She came home because her father is sick," Kate added.

The woman shook her head. "There's no one in Wittagar named Perl," she said, her voice flat, definite, and she turned and tromped off toward the kitchen.

We sat staring at one another. "She told me Wittagar," I said, for what felt like the tenth time.

I could tell from the look on Dave's face that he was beginning to doubt me, and the little spurt of courage that had brought Kate here seemed to have evaporated entirely.

"We have to keep looking," I said, trying to sound more confident than I was. "We've come all this way, and somebody will know how to find her. It's just a matter of asking the right person."

But then we sat in glum silence. No one seemed to have any idea of where that right person might be. By the time the waitress flapped back through the swinging kitchen doors, carrying our cheeseburgers and fries on thick platters, we had sunk into a three-way depression. She thumped the food down in front of us and then asked, her fists cocked on her hips, "By any chance would it be Mary Perlowski you're looking for?"

"Mary Perlowski?" I repeated stupidly. That was the name the operator had said, *Perlowski*.

"I got to thinking," the woman said. "I heard a while back that Mary'd had her name changed—at the court, you know. It might be she calls herself Perl now, maybe Meredith, too. She always was one for putting on airs."

"But why would she do that—change her name?" Kate asked.

The waitress shrugged extravagantly. It was obvious she thought people did a lot of things she couldn't be expected to account for. It was also obvious that, whoever Mary Perlowski was, this woman didn't like her very much.

"Mary sounds like the one you're asking about," she said. "She's a teacher, and her father's sick, like you said. Been that way a long time. He can't move nothing but his head since his tractor accident, five, six years ago."

We stared at one another, but no one could find anything to say.

"I can tell you where she lives, if she's the one you want," the waitress added, shifting her feet in a way that made it clear she wanted us to make up our minds so she could leave, maybe even sit down.

"Was she a teacher here?" I asked.

"Yeah," the waitress answered. "For a little while."

"It's got to be her," I said in response to Dave's incredulous look. "She told me she taught in Wittagar for a couple of years after she got fired at the *Chicago News*."

The waitress snorted abruptly, as though there was something funny about what I'd said. She started to turn away.

"Wait," I demanded, beginning to feel annoyed with the woman's attitude. "Tell us where she lives, please," I added as an afterthought, seeing a kind of irritated-mother look flash across her face.

Without a word, she bent over the table and drew us a simple map on a napkin. The house she was directing us to was only about two blocks away, but then everything seemed to be within two blocks of the middle of Main Street in Wittagar.

"What makes you so sure the woman she talked about is Ms. Perl?" Dave demanded when the waitress had gone through the swinging door into the kitchen again. "I can't see her being Mary Perlowski. I think you've got the whole thing wrong. I don't think she ever lived here."

"Unless you have a better suggestion," I told him, "I think we should check it out."

He had no better suggestion, apparently, because he said nothing, just picked up his cheeseburger, and started to eat. I did the same. Juice ran from my burger as I bit into it, but still, the first bite crumbled in my mouth like dust.

What would I find at Mary Perlowski's house?

. . .

"Yes?"

The porch light had flicked on in response to our knocking and a thin, stoop-shouldered woman with brownish gray hair held the storm door open a crack and peered at us.

"Excuse me, ma'am," I said, practically bowing in my effort to be polite, "but is your name Mrs. Perlowski?"

"Yes?" She looked from one to the other of us, a worried smile twisting the corners of her mouth.

"And do you have a daughter named Meredith Perl who teaches at East Junior High in the Cities?"

For a moment she looked at me as if she had never heard the name before, but then she said, recognition dawning, "Oh, it's Mary you want. I still haven't got used to that new name. Yes, she's here." Mrs. Perlowski didn't move, however. She just stood there, examining us quizzically, neither inviting us in nor sending us away, and we stood staring back. I suppose we were all trying to figure out what to say next.

"May we see her?" Dave asked, recovering himself first.

"See her? But I . . . well, yes. I guess you can. She's not feeling too well. That's why she came back. But if you're students of hers, I'm sure she'd want to see you." She opened the door just wide enough for us to enter, one at a time. "What are you children doing so far from home?"

"It's not so far," I defended. "She . . . Ms. Perl . . . Mary is our newspaper adviser at school. There's a . . . a problem, and we thought we'd better let her know."

In the dim hallway Mrs. Perlowski's skin looked like paper that had been crumpled and then smoothed out again. "A problem?" she repeated. "Oh dear, I hope Mary hasn't—"

"Who is it, Maude?" came a querulous voice from just beyond the wall.

Mrs. Perlowski rolled her eyes forlornly in the direction from which the voice had come. "It's some of Mary's pupils from her new school, Papa, come to see her. Nothing to worry your head about." Then to us she whispered, "Now you children stay right here. I'll go get Mary. And don't pay attention to anything he says. He makes a nuisance of himself sometimes." She disappeared up a stairway, leaving us standing in a tight little triangle in the hall.

"Come in here, won't you?" the voice demanded. "I can't see through walls."

We looked at one another, speechless, and finally it was Dave who turned his hands out expressively and stepped through the doorway into the next room.

"We didn't want to bother you," Dave said. "We're just waiting to see Ms. Perl . . . Mary."

"You by yourself? I thought Maude said 'some of Mary's pupils.' Is it only you?"

"No," Dave acknowledged, and as he spoke, Kate

and I came into the room behind him.

The voice was coming from a hospital bed, set in the middle of the living room. The top half of the bed was elevated slightly and a head of spiky white hair appeared above a tightly tucked-in sheet. There was hardly any indication of a body under the sheet except for two tent-pole-like projections that must have been feet. They jutted up at the bottom of the bed, a long distance from the head.

"Come closer," Mr. Perlowski said, his voice resonant and commanding despite the emaciated body it issued from. "I want to see you." He didn't move a muscle, but his eyes darted from one face to the other. His eyes were a startling, whitish blue, exactly like Ms. Perl's, and his nose was a hooked beak from which the rest of his face fell away.

Saying nothing, but bumping against one another and shuffling to slow our hesitant progress, we moved toward the bed.

"I'm Leslie Johnson," I said.

"And I'm Kate," Kate said. "Kate Connolly."

"Where are you kids from?" he asked looking us over as if the answer might be "the moon."

"East Junior High," I said. "Where your daughter teaches."

Mr. Perloswki studied me, seeming to see beneath my skin, another trait he shared with his daughter. "So you're the kids Mary ran off and left me for, huh?" he said at last.

"We're her students," Kate answered, when neither Dave nor I spoke. "She's the adviser for our newspaper."

He grunted. "Yeah. That's what I mean. Used to be Mary was here at night to help her mama. Since she's gone, that blasted county nurse comes in." He snorted, his nostrils flaring. "Horse-faced old woman! Can't stand her in the same room!"

I couldn't think of anything to say to that and apparently the others couldn't either, so we stood there by his bed like a row of department-store dummies, silent and waiting.

"How'd you get here?" Mr. Perlowski asked suddenly.

Dave replied, "We hitched."

The eyes in the bed snapped. "Pretty dumb, girls hitching rides."

"I'm not a girl," Dave said, scowling and sticking out his chest.

Mr. Perlowski looked Dave over. "You didn't introduce yourself," he said, "but you're little enough to be a girl. And it's hard to tell what's under that hat."

Dave reached up and pulled off his stocking hat, his bright green hair rising to attention as the hat was removed.

Mr. Perlowski stared, then let out a hoarse guffaw. "Put the hat back on," he said. "I'd keep my head covered, too, if I had grass growing out of the top."

Dave grinned and pulled his stocking cap back on.

Obviously Mr. Perlowski had passed the David Wiley character test.

"Who is it, Papa?" The question came from behind us, and we all froze where we stood, our backs to the familiar voice.

"You tell *me*, Mary. These kids say they belong to you," Mr. Perlowski answered. Something resembling a smile twitched at the corners of his mouth.

We turned then, one at a time, like dancers in a chorus line. Ms. Perl was standing in the doorway from the hall, wearing tight jeans and a sweater that wasn't too loose-fitting, either, her hair cascading around her shoulders in soft curls. When we were all facing her she didn't move, but continued to stand, her face expressionless, as if she hadn't yet seen anyone she knew.

"Hi," I said, and my voice came out like the piping of a baby bird. I folded my arms across my chest, a chill creeping over me.

Ms. Perl didn't acknowledge my greeting. The silence in the room was so heavy I could have reached out and touched it. Then, as if recognizing us at last, Ms. Perl smiled, kind of a half smile, not one that made her look especially happy, and said, "You know, it's funny, but I don't remember inviting you kids to my house."

Eleven

"He said what?" Ms. Perl leaned toward me across the kitchen table, her face like a hatchet.

"Dr. Schultz said *The Roving Reporter* is disbanded," I repeated.

Kate and Dave were sitting on each side of me, but they hadn't helped much with the explanations. Mrs. Perlowski stood in front of the stove, hands folded beneath her apron, her face creased into a puzzled frown. Ms. Perl's father—who was paralyzed, as the waitress had said, though he didn't seem particularly sick otherwise—remained in his hospital bed in the living room. When Ms. Perl had told him to go to sleep, he responded with a string of cheerful cuss words. The swearing didn't faze Ms. Perl, but her mother was clearly embarrassed. "Don't listen to him," she had commanded. "He doesn't mean anything he says."

Now Ms. Perl sat at the end of the table, biting her lip and considering the information I had given her. "There must be something I can do," she said at last.

I took a deep breath. She was going to help us! "What we thought was if you would go and see Mr. DeWitt, speak to him, you know, that you would be able to talk him out of resigning. If he comes back, then Dr. Schultz wouldn't have anything to be mad about." I tried on a smile, but Ms. Perl's expression didn't change. She was looking curiously blank.

"If anybody can talk him into changing his mind, you can," Dave added.

Ms. Perl scowled then. "Talk to Mr. DeWitt. *Apologize*, you mean?"

She made the word sound . . . well, almost dirty. I thought quickly and said, "Not exactly apologize. More just explain. Tell him about journalistic integrity, things like that."

Kate was nodding her agreement. "He would listen to you," she said.

"Apologies never change anything," Ms. Perl said, "and besides, I'm not going to go crawling to *him*."

"Mary," Mrs. Perlowski said, her voice plaintive, "you haven't been writing things to make people angry again, have you?"

"I haven't written anything," Ms. Perl snapped, without glancing in her mother's direction.

I could feel every hope we had come to Wittagar with draining away. "But . . . but . . . what else is there to do?" I asked.

Still Ms. Perl didn't seem to react.

"We thought you could convince him," Dave said, reaching out as though he were going to touch her, but then letting his hand drop and slide back to the edge of the table.

Ms. Perl had been twisting a long strand of her coppery hair. Now she tossed it over her shoulder and stood up, shoving her chair back so rapidly that it tipped. Her mother winced and reached out to catch the back of the chair to keep it from falling. Ms. Perl, not noticing either the chair or her mother, turned and began to pace. "I thought all this would have blown over by Monday morning," she said, pivoting in front of the old curved-top refrigerator.

Kate sat up straighter in her chair. "You mean you knew about Mr. DeWitt before you left?" she asked.

"Of course," Ms. Perl answered impatiently, reaching the wringer washing machine on the far side of the kitchen and turning again, starting back toward the refrigerator. "How could I have *not* known? The whole school was buzzing with the news."

"And that's why you left early . . . because you knew?" I asked. There was a curious feeling growing in my chest . . . almost as if I were suffocating on too much air.

Ms. Perl nodded abruptly, not bothering to look at me. "I figured if I wasn't there, Dr. Schultz wouldn't have anybody to take his wrath out on—"

"Except Leslie," Kate inserted softly, but Ms. Perl seemed not to have heard.

"And that by Monday the whole thing would be forgotten," she concluded.

"So you left," I said, dully. Dave shot me a penetrating look, but then returned to watching Ms. Perl's progress back and forth across the kitchen. I didn't know why I felt so . . . betrayed. If Ms. Perl had told me what she was going to do, if she had asked me to stand up to Dr. Schultz for her—or to a dragon, for that matter—I would have agreed instantly. But for her simply to go off without saying a word. . . . I didn't know what to say.

"I hadn't figured on his disbanding the paper." She tugged at her long hair. "If he discontinues the journalism class, I might get cut back to part time. Unless there's another class I could get."

I stood up. "You mean you're not even going to fight for it?"

Ms. Perl stopped to face me, her head high. "Of course, I'm going to fight! You don't think I'd take being put on part time without a fight, do you?"

"For the paper," I said. "For *The Roving Reporter.* Aren't you going to fight for that?"

"Oh," she said, understanding what I meant this time, and then she turned away. "I'll talk to Dr. Schultz, if that's what you mean."

"Talking to Dr. Schultz isn't going to help," I told her. "I know it won't. He's made up his mind. The only way is to get Mr. DeWitt to come back. He's the one you've got to talk to."

She shrugged. "If talking to Dr. Schultz doesn't help, then it doesn't. I wouldn't lower myself by crawling to DeWitt."

"But Ms. Perl!" I wailed.

"Come now, surely you don't expect me to lose face over a silly little school paper, do you?" She poured herself a mug of coffee.

I was reeling, and I reached out to the edge of the table for support. "You don't even care . . . about the paper or about us either!"

Ms. Perl turned back, the mug raised to her lips so that she peered at me through the steam. "I care about my job," she said mildly, "and if you were in my position, it's what you would care about too."

"Then why did you let my article go to press?" I demanded. "I asked you . . . I specifically *asked* you if what I'd written was too strong, if it pointed too directly at Mr. DeWitt, and you said it was all right. You said he should learn to see himself as he is."

Ms. Perl took a sip of coffee then, grimaced either at the taste or at the heat . . . or maybe at me . . . and lowered the mug just enough so I could see the way her lips turned down at the corners. "I said nothing of the kind, Leslie. If you will recall, I was busy when you came in with that article. I told you to leave it, but you wouldn't."

For a moment, I couldn't catch my breath. Dave and Kate were both staring at me, Dave accusing, Kate in complete bewilderment. "That's a lie," I said at last, stepping in closer to Ms. Perl, staggering almost. "That's a complete lie. You read my article. I stood there and watched while you read it."

Her frown deepened. She turned to the others. "Did you see anything like that, Dave? Did you, Kate?"

Dave shook his head. Kate simply sat there, mute.

"But they weren't there!" I shouted. "Nobody was there but you and me!"

Ms. Perl's eyes narrowed, glitteringly blue. She reminded me of Aslan when he was about to attack. "Then I guess it's your word against mine, isn't it," she said. It wasn't a question.

I was near tears, my voice shaking. "I came in before school," I reminded her, "and you were grading papers—recording grades in your grade book, anyway—and I asked you to read my article."

Ms. Perl was nodding, agreeing at last.

"I asked you," I repeated.

"And I said I was busy. I told you to leave it."

"But I said . . . I said that I wanted you to read it then, so if anything was wrong, I could rewrite it during the day. And you . . . you did!" My hands were trembling. In fact, I was shaking all over.

Ms. Perl reached out and touched my cheek, her hand cool and dry. "I may have glanced at it, but, *you know* I didn't have time then to read it. You said yourself—it was before school, I was busy recording grades."

"But I *asked* you specifically about the part about Mr. DeWitt. You looked at it again. You even said—"

Ms. Perl cut me off then, let her hand drop. "I did nothing of the kind."

"But . . ." I stammered.

She smiled, almost kindly. "Leslie, it's time you learned to take responsibility for your own mistakes."

I sank into a chair, speechless.

"But Ms. Perl—" Kate started to say.

Dave was nodding his head vigorously, watching Ms. Perl with adoring eyes. "You took the consequences when you were fired from the *Chicago News*, didn't you? And now we have to do the same thing."

At the mention of the *Chicago News*, Mrs. Perlowski gasped, her hands flying to her mouth. But before she had a chance to speak, Ms. Perl whirled to face her. "Mother," she warned, her voice low, "don't you say a word!"

Mrs. Perlowski shook her head, her hands still covering her mouth and her eyes round above them. "Why did you tell them such a thing, Mary?" she asked, plaintively. "You know you never—"

Ms. Perl slammed her cup down next to the stove, slopping coffee onto the counter and down the front of the cupboard onto the floor. She stepped toward her mother, her chin thrust forward like a battering ram. "You're going to ruin it for me, aren't you? You're going to ruin everything."

"I can't let you lie to these children," her mother said, shrilly. "You've never even been to Chicago, let alone worked—"

"Shut up!" Ms. Perl's cheeks flamed brighter than her hair, and she stood so close that she nearly forced her mother backwards over the stove. "You just shut up!"

Kate paled and even Dave looked shocked. Apparently Ms. Perl had gone farther than she had intended, because she retreated suddenly, giving her mother room to straighten up. Ms. Perl turned away from us, her back rigid. For a moment I thought she was crying, but when she faced her mother again, her eyes were dry and her face was stony cold.

"Do you want to know why I made that up . . . about being a reporter on the *Chicago News?*" she asked. "So I could get out of this stinking hole, that's why. So I could live my own life for once instead of yours . . . and *his!*" She flung one arm in the direction of the living room where her father lay.

Mrs. Perlowski flinched as though she had been slapped and was expecting another blow.

"'You can't leave me, Mary. I can't manage your daddy alone,'" Ms. Perl mimicked in a high, whining voice.

"It's hard," Mrs. Perlowski said. "You've no idea how hard. He listens to you."

Ms. Perl broke in on top of her mother's words. "I know how hard. I was back here every night, wasn't I . . . every damned night, even through college? I took a job here when everybody else had moved on to bigger and better things."

"I always thought you liked your job at the school, Mary." Mrs. Perlowski's voice quavered.

"Hah!" It was more an exclamation than a laugh. "Do you want to know something? The first stroke of luck I ever had in my life was getting fired from that school. It gave me a chance to start over . . . everything new!"

Mrs. Perlowski looked past Ms. Perl to us and said, her voice confiding and gentle. "Mary used to write for *The Wittagar Weekly* in her spare time. Lovely articles. People here often spoke to me about them." She twisted her apron in her hands, smoothed it again. "But then she started to write bad things . . . about the newspaper . . . about the school. Everyone was upset with her. The whole town!"

"When I see a pile of crap," Ms. Perl said, "I call it a pile of crap, and if people don't like it, they can shove—"

"Mary!" her mother said, shocked, and Ms. Perl shrugged her shoulders, turned away.

She looked at us as if she were surprised to find us still there. "Go home," she said flatly. "Go back and tell them everything you've heard. You might as well make it easy for Dr. Schultz. He can disband me along with your silly newspaper. My mother will be delighted."

"We wouldn't . . ." I started to say, but then I stopped and looked at Dave and Kate. I didn't know what we would do. Dave's face was lopsided. He seemed caught between amazement and grief, and even Kate looked stricken. It didn't matter, though, because Ms. Perl left the room without waiting to hear what I was going to say. We could hear her footsteps moving up the inside stairs . . . heavy and slow.

Mrs. Perlowski dabbed her eyes with the corner of her apron, and then took out a sponge from beneath the sink, wet it, and busied herself cleaning up the spilled coffee. She knelt on the floor, wiping the face of the drawers, neither speaking nor looking in our direction.

I stood up, steadying myself with my hands. Mrs. Perlowski glanced up from her work.

"I'd like to use your telephone if I may," I said. "I'll call collect. My mom will come to get us. She told me to call if I needed a ride."

Twelve

My mother didn't ask what we thought we were doing, following a teacher fifty miles to her home; she just said she would be there to get us as soon as she could. That's my mother— come to the rescue now, ask for explanations later. I guess when it's me being rescued, I don't mind the way she is at all.

Mrs. Perlowski made us tea and cinnamon toast. We told her we had already eaten, but she said, "Kids can always eat," and continued buttering the toast with quick, jabbing motions. She served the food silently and, instead of sitting down with us at the table while we ate, she stood at her place in front of the stove, folding and unfolding her hands.

"I'm sorry," I said after I had eaten the last crumbs of toast and Mrs. Perlowski had gathered our cups. "We didn't mean to cause trouble."

"I guess Mary causes her own trouble," Mrs. Perlowski said, and she turned on the faucet fiercely to run hot water into the sink.

. . .

When my mother came to the door an hour or so later, she was wearing a yellow stocking hat that had been mine when I was a little girl and a pair of mismatched gloves and an old coat of my father's that left her wrists looking bony and bare.

I looked her over and waited for the familiar feeling, half embarrassment, half protectiveness, to rise in my chest, but it didn't come. I was simply glad she was there. I didn't know whether that meant I was growing up or if I was reverting to the little girl who wouldn't feel safe if she admitted her mother was less than perfect.

Mrs. Perlowski had followed Dave and Kate and me to the door, but Ms. Perl didn't come down from upstairs.

We stood around in the hallway, and I kept looking up the stairs, thinking she would come . . . that she would apologize or explain or . . . I guess I didn't know what she could do, but I wanted her to do it anyway.

"They're nice children," Mrs. Perlowski told my mother.

"Yes, they are," my mother agreed, smiling at us warmly.

I'll bet Mr. DeWitt thinks so, too, I said to myself.

I looked back as we went out the door, and I could see into the living room. Mr. Perlowski's head was turned toward us. I wasn't certain, but I thought he was watching from the darkened room. I wondered if he had heard everything that had been said that evening.

From outside I looked to the upstairs window. There was no light, no sign of movement. Ms. Perl might never have existed . . . except for the tight, heavy feeling that seemed to have taken up permanent residence where my stomach was supposed to be.

We piled into the car, Dave and Kate in back and me in front with my mother, and headed east on Highway 12.

"Well, Leslie?" my mother asked, after we had been driving in silence for about ten minutes.

I sighed, though I knew if I'd been her, I wouldn't have lasted that long waiting for explanations. I told her . . . about Mr. DeWitt quitting, the newspaper being disbanded, about asking Ms. Perl to come back to talk to him. "She's not going to apologize," I said in conclusion. "She said she won't talk to Mr. DeWitt at all."

"She's too proud," Dave justified from the backseat, but he didn't sound exactly happy.

"Anyway," I told my mother, "you were right."

"About what?" she asked, a small edge of hopefulness in her voice.

"About toothpaste," I said.

She nodded. The green lights from the dash lighted up the lower half of her face, making her look skeletal, almost witchlike. The good witch of the north, I thought.

"How did you get to be the way you are?" I asked, thinking about role models. "I mean, was your mom the earth-mother type?"

"My mother?" She glanced at me, then looked quickly back at the highway again. "No. My mother had too many kids and too much work to do. Her health was never good after the last two. I always had the feeling when I was growing up that she used to wish she could put us back."

"Back? Back where?"

"Anywhere we'd fit, I suppose." Mom laughed, but the laugh seemed a little sad.

"But how does that explain you?"

"You mean my compulsive mothering?" She smiled. "It's a reaction, maybe, trying to give what I always wanted and never had." She turned to study my face, and I found myself looking away. "Why do you ask?" Her voice was soft.

"I just wondered," I said.

We rode in silence, then, the darkened prairie skimming by on either side of the car.

When I thought about Ms. Perl, the thought was a kind of ache. She had lied. More than just the lie to get the job. I could understand that, I guess, though I knew I couldn't have done it. But she had lied to me for no reason at all about not having checked my article. It wasn't even the kind of lie that might have saved her skin. It had accomplished nothing, except to make her look better in front of Dave and Kate and her mother for a moment. Only a moment.

The trip home seemed shorter than the one going. I don't know why it is, but that often seems true. Maybe home is always closer to us than any other place. We dropped Dave off before we went on to our street. I discovered that he lives in a concrete high rise, one of those subsidized apartment complexes for low-income families.

"Thank you, Mrs. Johnson," he said, very formally, before he got out. And then he reached forward and touched my shoulder. "I just want you to know, Leslie," he said, "that I believe you."

"Leslie always tells the truth," Kate said quietly. "Even sometimes when you wish she wouldn't."

Kate and Dave both smiled at me, so I smiled back.

. . .

That night I dreamed about Mr. DeWitt. He was writing algebraic equations on the board, but every time he turned around to face the board, the class laughed. Somebody—was it me?—had pinned a sign to his back that said KICK ME!

And then everything changed, the way it can in dreams. I don't know where I was, but Dave was kissing me. It was a long kiss. Electricity traveled from my toes all the way to my scalp. Only when he finished I looked down and saw he was standing on a ladder in order to reach me. I couldn't help it; I laughed, and the dream-Dave disappeared.

In his place there was Ms. Perl, and she was laughing too. Her laughter cut through me like a knife.

When I got up, I was more tired than I had been when I went to bed. "There's nothing wrong," I told myself. "Nothing to worry about. If Ms. Perl loses her job because Mr. DeWitt has resigned, it's only fair."

But somehow, I wasn't sure fair was the issue for either Ms. Perl or Mr. DeWitt.

When I got downstairs, my mother was sitting at the kitchen table checking the grocery ads in the paper and making out a list. One of the cats was sitting in her lap, a part Persian with a black patch over one eye named Long John Silver. He reached up every now and then to take a lazy swipe at her pencil.

"Oh, *you!*" she said to Long John, but she didn't put him off her lap.

Aslan was curled on the kitchen counter, absorbing the heat from the electric coffeepot. I reached out to pet him, and he opened his triangular pink mouth and hissed. I pushed him off the counter onto the floor.

"Do you want some breakfast?" Mother asked. "I've got blueberry muffins keeping warm in the oven."

I opened the oven door and peered in. "What do they have in them—besides blueberries, I mean?"

She pretended to be indignant. "They're straight from the recipe book . . . almost."

"What's the almost?" I asked, studying them. They looked a bit nubbly, apart from the blueberries, even.

"Well, I did add half a cup of Grape Nuts to the batter." Mother smiled apologetically.

I got out the butter and milk, piled a plate with hot muffins, Grape Nuts and all. "Where's Dad?" I asked. "And Brian?" I flopped into the chair across from my mother.

"Dad's taking Brian to a basketball clinic."

I nodded, trying to think of something else neutral to say. When nothing came to me, I finally said, "I've been thinking. If anybody's going to apologize to Mr. DeWitt, I guess it's going to have to be me."

Mom said nothing, but her eyebrows had that special arch they get when she's feeling encouraged but trying not to say too much in case I change my mind.

"Only . . ." I stopped, picked out a blueberry, and ate it.

"Only?" my mother repeated, when I didn't continue.

"I can't," I said, setting the muffin down again. "I just can't face him. I mean, if you'd seen the way he looked, you would know . . ."

"Maybe a telephone call would be easier," she said.

"Yeah." I sagged in the seat. "I suppose it would be." I waited for my mother to say something more, something I could get annoyed about, maybe, and then I could use her as an excuse for not calling. She's getting smarter in her old age, though; she didn't say a word. "Is Mr. DeWitt in the phone book, do you suppose?" I asked at last.

"I would expect so," she answered, returning to her grocery list as if the whole thing had nothing to do with her.

I just sat there, watching her. Her list was in three sections according to the sales at three different stores. I had never noticed before that my mother was so organized. I read a bit of her upside-down list: celery—she would probably put that in scrambled eggs—milk, raisins, guava paste. What on earth was *guava paste?*

"I think you would feel better, Leslie, if you talked to him," she said after a while. "I know I would if I were you."

"Well, you're not me," I said, narrowing my eyes at Aslan, who was on the counter next to the coffeepot again. He stared back at me out of cobalt-blue eyes, mark of some forgotten Siamese ancestor.

"No, I'm not you," my mother said, adding something I couldn't read to her list, "and you're not me. You are uniquely yourself."

For a moment I continued to sit, slumped in my chair on my side of the table. Then I got up and headed for the telephone book in the hall.

Thirteen

When I picked up the telephone receiver, it seemed so heavy in my hand that I wasn't sure I was going to be able to hold it to my ear. I dialed slowly, awkwardly, rechecking the number three times. At the other end, the telephone began to ring—two, three, four times. *Maybe,* I encouraged myself, *no one is home.*

But then the ringing stopped, and a cheerful, grandmotherly sounding "Hello" came over the line.

For a moment I was so certain I had a wrong number that I couldn't respond. It had never occurred to me that Mr. DeWitt was married. Actually, I suppose I had never thought of him as having a life outside of school.

"Hel——hello? Is this Mr. DeWitt's house?" I asked.

"Yes," came the reply.

"The Mr. DeWitt who teaches algebra at East Junior High?"

"Yes," she said again, "it is."

"Uh . . . I'd like to speak to him, please."

"May I tell him who's calling?" the woman asked, which caught me off guard. I hadn't expected that. Surely she would have seen the article, my name on the article, or heard Mr. DeWitt talk about me. I was going to have to identify myself to him, of course, but somehow I didn't want *her* to know.

"Uh . . ." I said, "uh . . . this is Leslie Johnson."

A brief silence followed in which I could hear nothing but a light, vibrating hum on the line, and then Mrs. DeWitt must have collected herself because she said, "Just a moment, Leslie. I'll get him." I could hear the phone being laid down and her calling, "Charles."

Charles. So he had a first name. I had never thought about that, either.

I waited, my palm sweating so much that I had to change the receiver to the other hand twice, wiping my palm on my jeans, before Mr. DeWitt's voice came on the line.

"Leslie?"

"Yes," I said, but then I couldn't think of what I had been going to say. I should have written it all out before I picked up the phone, I guess, but I just stood there with my tongue tied into a thousand knots.

After a long wait, Mr. DeWitt spoke again. "What's red and grows around the house?" he asked.

I staggered a little, as if I had been hit, but finally I managed to ask, "What did you say?"

"What's red and grows around the house?" he repeated.

I leaned against the wall. "I don't know."

"Grass" came the reply. "I was lying about the color."

"Ha," I said. "Ha, ha, ha." I could feel the breath I hadn't known I was holding slipping out of my lungs with each feeble laugh. The man could still tell dumb jokes. Maybe he was indestructible.

And then there was silence again.

"That's good," I said, at last. "That was a good one."

Another pause, and then I remembered that *I* was the one who had made the call, that he was waiting for me.

"Mr. DeWitt," I said, "I want to apologize . . . about the article I wrote." That was a start, at least, but it wasn't enough, and I didn't know what else there was to say. I wouldn't be honest if I told him I hadn't meant what I'd written.

"That's kind of you, Leslie," he said. "I won't pretend your article wasn't upsetting, because it was, but I thought your writing showed promise."

I couldn't stand it. It was like being praised for performing an execution well. "I'm sorry, Mr. DeWitt," I said. "I really am sorry. I guess I just didn't think . . ."

"Don't be sorry, Leslie. I humiliated you, and you paid me back. I had it coming."

"But it wasn't the same," I said, "my article and your calling me in front of the class. Besides, I wasn't paying attention that day."

"Never mind," he said, his voice getting very soft so I had to hold my breath to hear, "I've known for a long time."

"Known?" I repeated, like some kind of echo.

"That the kids make fun of me, that I'm not a very good teacher."

What could I say? *Oh no, Mr. DeWitt. You're the best teacher I've ever had. All those things I wrote were lies?*

"Only . . ." His voice might have been static on the line. "Only I want you to know one thing."

"What's that?"

"When I make mistakes on the board? In the problems?"

"Yes?"

"I'm not stupid, not *that* stupid anyway. I can do the problems."

"Then why—?"

"Why do I act so dumb? It was just my way of trying to keep you kids on your toes, helping you feel competent. Catch the teacher out, you know? But you see . . ." His voice trailed off, and I thought for a moment he wasn't going to finish. Actually, I wished he wouldn't, but I couldn't think of anything to say to stop him.

"When I was a kid in school"—the sound in the telephone receiver was like a mosquito buzzing in my ear—"I had a math teacher who used to make all us kids feel *dumb*. Me, too, and I always liked math. Lots of the people who went through that teacher's class probably never looked at a number for the rest of their lives without feeling incompetent. When I started to teach, back in the Stone Age," he let out a brief, brittle laugh, "I knew exactly what I wanted. I wanted school . . . I wanted *math* to be fun. It didn't matter so much if the kids liked me, but I wanted them to feel good, to go out of my class confident and strong. I guess over the years I got to acting the fool and didn't even notice what was happening."

"Oh no, Mr. DeWitt. That's all wrong!" I cried.

"Leslie, you started out telling the truth. Don't lie now. It's too late for that."

I don't know what you are supposed to say when somebody, especially an adult, especially one of your teachers, says something like that. Are you supposed to compliment them on their insight? I stood there staring at the hall wallpaper, wishing I were somebody else, someplace else, doing something else. My eyes were burning.

"Won't you come back, Mr. DeWitt?" I begged. "Dr. Schultz told me you resigned. I didn't mean for you to do that."

He didn't answer at first, and I waited, chewing on the inside of my cheek. Maybe he would come back. Not to help Ms. Perl. I figured she would take care of herself. Not even to keep *The Roving Reporter* functioning, though that would be nice. But for himself, because teaching was important to him. I guess I was hoping it was possible to retrieve a little bit of toothpaste from the bottom of the sink, despite what I knew.

"I appreciate your asking, Leslie, but no. I don't believe I will. I think it is obvious that I have stayed on too long. I have some other plans, anyway. A business my wife and I have been talking about starting for a long time." He paused. "Actually, I should thank you." His voice was very soft.

"Thank me," I repeated, and then I began to laugh—and sob—at the ridiculousness of the whole thing.

"Now, now, none of that, Leslie," Mr. DeWitt said, coming in strong again like a radio that has been turned up.

But I couldn't respond. I was crying too hard to say anything at all.

"Leslie? Leslie?"

I held the receiver away from my ear, trying to catch my breath, trying to stop, and I heard a tiny voice saying, "Do you know what's yellow and comes in trunks?"

I returned the receiver to my ear, shaking my head, no, though I don't know what I was expecting to communicate. Maybe I figured he could hear my brain rattle.

"What's yellow and comes in trunks?" he repeated, as though that would help, but then without waiting for me he gave the answer. "Elephant snot," and he giggled, just exactly the way he always used to giggle in class. I could almost see his jowls wobbling.

"Mr. DeWitt!" I cried, shocked, and then I was giggling too.

. . .

My mother was folding her list when I came back into the kitchen. "Are you all right?" she asked.

I nodded, wiping my eyes on my sweat-shirt sleeve. "Do you know what he did? He thanked me. He actually thanked me!"

"For what?" my mother asked, though she didn't look surprised.

"I don't know. For making him see his mistakes as a teacher, I guess." I sank into my chair. "He won't come back, though. He says he has 'other plans,' some kind of business he and his wife want to start. I don't know if he really does or not."

Aslan jumped down from his place by the coffee-pot and stalked across the floor, his tail swaying rhythmically. He wove between Mother's ankles and then headed for mine. I considered pushing him away, but didn't.

"I'm proud of you, Leslie," my mother said.

I looked at her, incredulous. "How could you be?"

She smiled then, and I noticed she had put on lipstick that morning, something she rarely does, but I also saw that she hadn't gotten it on very straight. "Easily," she answered. "You are honest, for one thing."

"Honest!" I repeated. "Big deal."

Aslan jumped up onto my lap, landing lightly. He bumped his hard, triangular head against my chin, and when I bent down to him, he pressed his cool nose to my nostrils, purring loudly.

"And you are loyal. I'm sure Ms. Perl must appreciate that."

I didn't say anything, just stroked Aslan. He kneaded my lap, preparing a good bed.

"You are also willing to own up to your mistakes," she continued. "That takes real maturity. There are some adults who never learn to do that."

Yes, there are, I agreed inwardly, thinking of my last encounter with Ms. Perl.

Aslan circled two, then three times and lay down, curled into a black ball with his nose tucked beneath his tail. His startling blue eyes studied my face for a moment, then drifted shut.

"But most important," my mother said, reaching across the table and touching my hand tentatively, as though she thought I might pull away, "you are kind."

Kind! I thought. *Kind?*

But then I looked at her, really looked at her . . . at the wings of graying hair that flare out on each side of her face, at the laugh lines radiating like sunbeams from her eyes, at a certain softness around her mouth that seemed to need some kind of response.

I smiled back at her and laid my other hand on top of hers, just lightly.

"Thanks," I said.

About the Author

Marion Dane Bauer lives in Minnetonka, Minnesota, with her husband, a son and a daughter, two dogs, two cats, and an array of visitors. She teaches fiction writing through the University of Minnesota's Continuing Education program and is the author of four previous novels for Clarion including *Rain of Fire*, winner of the 1984 Jane Addams Children's Book Award.

Having been a yearbook editor, a school newspaper advisor, a high school teacher, a mother, and a daughter, the author was able to draw from her own life experiences in writing this book. "Leslie's mother is a little like me," Ms. Bauer says, "though I am a less 'creative' cook and a more mundane dresser than she, and have yet to give artificial respiration to a cat."

25337

FIC
BAU

Bauer, Marion Dane.

Like mother, like
daughter.